Tales of the Were
Jaguar Island 2

The Jaguar Bodyguard

BIANCA D'ARC

This book is a work of fiction. The names, characters, places, and incidents are products of the writer's imagination or have been used fictitiously and are not to be construed as real. Any resemblance to persons, living or dead, actual events, locale or organizations is entirely coincidental.

No part of this book may be used or reproduced in any manner whatsoever without written permission, except in the case of brief quotations embodied in critical articles and reviews.

Sworn to protect his Clan, Nick Balam heads to Hollywood to keep an eye on a rising star who has seen too much for her own good. She saw a young jaguar shifter transforming and may have damning evidence that could expose them all to the world. It's up to Nick, as head of security for the Jaguar Clan to assess the situation and take care of the problem.

Unexpected fame has made a circus of Sullivan Lane's life, but when decapitated squirrels show up on her doorstep, she knows she needs professional help. Nick is able to insinuate himself into her security team. The only problem is... once he gets close to her, he realizes she might very well be his mate. And she's in danger. His mission expands to keeping her safe, catching her stalker and then figuring out what she intends to do about her newfound knowledge of shifters. And if she has proof – he's going to have to destroy it, which could destroy any trust between them.

Sparks fly and passions rise. Can he keep her safe and prevent her from revealing what she knows? Or will he have to forsake his Clan to find true happiness with a woman of rare beauty and...magic?

DEDICATION

This book is dedicated to my Dad, who puts up with my crazy hours and never complains. Even though he's never read any of my romance books, he is my biggest cheerleader, always encouraging me to keep writing and keep persevering. I love you, Dad.

And to my readers and friends. Particularly Peggy McChesney and Jessica Bimberg, proofreader and editor, respectively. They've helped me so much over these past few years. You gals are great!

CHAPTER 1

Nick Balam was on special assignment for his newly mated Alpha, billionaire Mark Pepard. Nick didn't like being away from the safety of the Clan or unable to keep tabs on the Alpha. As Beta of the Clan, it was his responsibility to make sure the Alpha came to no harm. Ever.

But Nick also had a duty to obey the Alpha, and right now, Mark had convinced Nick that he could best serve the interests of the Clan by being here. In Hollywood. Watching over a human starlet who might have learned more than she should have about the Clan and their secrets. Nick was here to assess the situation—and the girl—and see if she needed to be silenced permanently.

It wasn't something Nick would do lightly, but to protect his Clan, he would do more than kill. He would lay down his life for the Clan, if need be. Arranging an *accident* for a single human was a small thing compared to the allegiance he owed his people in their bid to make a new life for themselves on Jaguar Island.

For the Jaguar Clan was rebuilding. Slowly. They'd been decimated by the drug wars and the lack of a strong, central gathering place where they could seek shelter in numbers. Living as wild cats, each with their own private territory, hadn't worked out well as drug cartels moved in on the

1

jungles the jaguars had called home. So many had been slaughtered, caught up in the senseless killing and violence, each trying to drive the interlopers from their territories.

It was Mark Pepard who had finally put forward a plan and, with approval of the remaining elders, put it into motion. He'd purchased an island in the Caribbean—a dormant volcano that spoke to the fire of the jaguar that lived inside them all. He'd also found an architect, who turned out to be his mate, to design a community that his people could live in together, and grow.

For the first time, Nick thought they might actually have a chance at rebuilding the might of the Jaguar Clan and adapting to the brave new world the humans had created. So much, though, depended on secrecy. And the actress, Sullivan Lane, had seen and heard things she should never have been allowed to witness.

At least, that's what Nick was here to investigate. He was deep undercover, acting as Sullivan's bodyguard, watching her every move and doing his best to discover if she had knowledge that needed to be erased. Which would, of course, mean *erasing* her. Permanently.

So far, she hadn't given any indication that she'd go running to the tabloids with her story or the proof they thought she might have. It was Nick's job to, first, see if she did have the feared evidence of the existence of jaguar shifters, and second, if she did, to make sure she never got a chance to pass it on to anyone else. Above all, their secret must be maintained.

Sullivan was a lot different than he'd expected. He had met her only briefly. Introduced by her manager as the replacement for another bodyguard who had been contracted only recently to see to the up-and-coming actress's safety. She'd been receiving death threats ever since her new movie had opened last week.

It had been the night of the premiere that she'd been involved in a situation that had let the cat out of the bag—almost literally. One of their younger and much more foolish

Clan members had been working as a valet, parking cars at the director's mansion at an exclusive after-party that had a guest list in the hundreds. Only a teenager, Rafael hadn't fully mastered his jaguar yet, which normally wouldn't have been that much of a problem, except that one of the other youngsters had been showing off and lost control of a very expensive vehicle, nearly hitting Rafael in the middle of the dark parking area.

Rafael had not only jumped clear of the oncoming car, but in his panic, his cat had come out. The poor kid had shifted in mid-air, then been unable to shift back because of the panic and fear that had made his animal a little crazy. The other kids had tried to talk him down. They were Clan members, too. But none of them had realized until it was almost too late that Sullivan had come out to get her car and had probably seen the entire episode. She had her phone in her hands, and they couldn't be sure she hadn't taken video of Rafael's change.

Rafael and his folks had been given one-way tickets to Jaguar Island, where the teen could learn to better control his inner cat with others his age. The elders there would help him, too, and if he shifted in public, nobody would care because every single person on that island was a trusted Clan member. It was a place where they could let their jaguars run free without fear.

So unlike the human world, where they had to watch their every step. This little incident could blow up in their faces if not handled properly. Nick was the expert in the Clan when it came to security and protection. Mark might be Alpha, but in their culture, the Alpha was the big-picture position. The Alpha had to dream the dream that kept the rest of the Clan on track. He was the leader, but each member of his support staff had their own important functions.

Nick was the Beta, which meant he headed all security for the Clan. When it came to protection of their personnel and their secrets, Nick was the leader. The Alpha of the Clan's security team, as it were.

When a human had witnessed a shift, it could usually be explained away by the introduction of drugs or alcohol, which was a much nicer way to lead an unsuspecting human to believe they'd been seeing things. But, when there might be actual evidence, that was a high-priority security breach. The fact that they weren't sure and couldn't just go rifling through Sullivan Lane's home or personal effects without triggering her own security brought it to the level where Nick had to be called in to preserve the best interests of the Clan as a whole.

He'd finagled his way onto her security team by calling in more than one favor from acquaintances he'd made over the years. The fact that Sullivan's star was on the rise with the release of her new film meant that she was more protected than she ever had been. The death threats that had accompanied her new-found fame had led her—very sensibly, if somewhat inconveniently—to hire a full-coverage security team from one of the best companies in the business.

Luckily, Nick had contacts in the company and was able to get his friends to shuffle a few things so he could join the team already in place. A human guy who'd been unhappy with the gig was taken off the team, and Nick was put in charge of the night shift—a perfect placement that would allow him to do a little covert snooping in the starlet's home while there on legitimate duty.

If she had video evidence of Rafael's shift, Nick would find it.

*

The new guy on the security team made Sal want to purr. He was fit and handsome in a way she hadn't expected. All the other guards looked like bulked-up gorillas to her, but the new guy—Nick was his name—was all sleek lines and graceful motion. He was big and burly, too, but in a way that reminded her of a sinuous dancer...or a jungle cat.

That thought gave her pause.

She knew she'd seen something she wasn't supposed to

see when she'd left the after-party at the director's mansion early. She'd seen a young man turn into a leopard. Or a jaguar. Something with spots and big scary teeth and claws. He'd scurried into the shadows, but the wide-eyed fear on his friends' faces when they saw her standing there was enough to tell her that the boys were all in on the secret that their friend was hiding a powerful magic in his teenaged body.

Sal knew a little about magic from her mother, but not enough to really know what she'd seen. She knew enough to keep her mouth shut, though. One did *not* talk about magic, unless one wanted to be committed and put in a room with padded walls and no windows.

Like her mother.

Being labeled crazy was something Sal wanted to avoid at all costs. If she'd had a chance to talk to the boys, she would have told them their secret was safe with her, but they'd all disappeared, leaving her to find her car on her own that night. Luckily, it hadn't been far away, and she'd been able to leave without a lot of fuss. She hadn't wanted to make a big production out of her departure from the party that had been getting increasingly wild.

When the drugs had come out, she'd made her exit. Cocaine had been passed around on mirrored platters like hors d'oevres, and pills in every color of the rainbow had been displayed like candy. It had made Sal uncomfortable, and rather than say anything that might get her ostracized from the crowd that could easily dictate whether she ever worked on another film again, she'd just left. Quietly. She'd just used a touch of the magic she never openly acknowledged to make herself disappear.

They gave her mother all kinds of drugs in that place. They'd dulled her mind so much that her mother rarely even recognized Sal when she found the courage to visit. The drugs had just about destroyed her mother's mind, quieting her wild magic and making her a docile shell of the woman she'd once been.

Of course, her mother had been violent. The magic hadn't

been a fuzzy, soft friend. It had been a harsh roar of passion that demanded attention and lashed out when it wasn't given what it wanted. The violence was what had gotten her mother sentenced to that place. A home for the criminally insane.

The shame and horror of it was what had first driven Sal to change her name. The need to hide her origins and reinvent herself over and over had led to a career as an actress. She knew her existence as Sullivan Lane, flavor-of-the-month, could be even shorter lived than usual if her secret got out. Sally Lannier could be dug up any old time and used to blackmail or discredit her reincarnation as Sullivan.

In a way, Sal hadn't really wanted the new movie to get such good reviews or critical acclaim. Being a star had drawbacks enough for a normal person, but with her background and the skeletons hiding in her closet, Sal would have been better off if she hadn't risen so far, so fast. A good, steady job was all she'd wanted. Now, she had to deal with fame and death threats because the subject matter of her last film had apparently touched a nerve among some of the more unstable elements of society.

The movie had been about a fictionalized account of a real-life serial killer case, and Sal had played the female detective who had cracked the case and almost become one of the victims herself. Sal had met with the detective—Elaine Mercado—and talked to her about her experiences working on that case and others. It had helped Sal get a feel for the role she had never expected to launch her into stardom, but that's just what had happened.

And now, someone was stalking her, much as Detective Mercado had been stalked by the real-life Lewiston Strangler twenty years ago. Sal hoped the person stalking her wasn't going to live out the entire fantasy and start killing people, but the tokens he'd been leaving for her ever since she'd taken on the role had been escalating. The last straw had been a decapitated squirrel, left on her front doorstep the day after opening night.

The idea that the stalker had gotten that close had

frightened Sal into upgrading her security. The team she'd had in place for about a week now had been good, but the night shift supervisor had been replaced with the new guy. Nick. Too short a name for a man like that. She wondered if that was short for Nicholas, or some other more exotic variant.

And she was spending way too much time thinking about her new bodyguard.

Sal got out of bed and padded downstairs to the kitchen. It was the middle of the night, but she couldn't sleep. Maybe a hot cup of tea would help.

Nick came to alert the moment he heard her get out of bed. His superior jaguar hearing allowed him to put away the papers he'd been examining in her desk and make it look as if he'd never spent the past hour snooping in her study. He went back to his security station in the front foyer of the large house, checking the camera feeds behind the little desk that had been installed to hold them.

The house was a rental, which made it easier in some ways to protect since it had already been wired for top-notch security when they'd moved her highness in a week ago. In fact, the security company had decided where to put her after a stalker put a dead squirrel on the front doorstep of her previous residence.

Good move, taking her away from a site that had already been compromised. Nick would have advised the same, had he been on the case last week. The new house had been rented furnished, which meant Sullivan Lane had only a few of her personal items here. He'd already perused the inventory lists from the moving company they'd hired to move her in four hours flat. The security company had coordinated that, as well, screening, hiring and overseeing the movers who did the actual work.

Fame and fortune could buy all sorts of services in this town, it seemed. Nick hadn't spent a lot of time on this coast, but he was familiar with the area from several trips he'd made while he'd been a young adventurer hell bent on seeing the world. He'd done his traveling mostly on Uncle Sam's dime as a Special Operator. The reputation, friends and contacts he'd made, then, had stood him in good stead all his life, including on this most recent mission.

He heard Sullivan come down the staircase in her slippers and head for the gourmet kitchen. It wouldn't be out of character for him to check in on her. He was supposed to be keeping watch inside the house at night, after all. He'd be a pretty piss-poor guard if he didn't check on the noise in the kitchen. Or so he told himself.

His decision had nothing at all to do with the fact that Sullivan Lane was one of the most attractive females he'd ever seen. Nope. No, siree. Not at all.

He peered around the corner into the kitchen doorway and stopped in his tracks. Her scent wrapped around him as it had earlier that day when he'd first met her. Warm cinnamon and spice. Like a holiday fruitcake he wanted to gobble up.

Whoa. Down, kitty.

"Everything okay, Miss Lane?"

Nick tried not to notice that his voice had come out in a deep rumble that meant his jaguar was very near the surface. Kitty was riled by the luscious scent of the woman, and his human side definitely noticed the way she filled out her clingy silk nightgown and whisper-thin robe.

She startled and whirled to face him, one hand going to cover her heart. Her eyes were wide with alarm until she recognized him in the doorway. He hadn't meant to scare her. He was glad when relief replaced fear in her deep blue gaze.

"Sorry, you scared me. I'm just making some tea. Want a cup?"

Her invitation surprised him. Wasn't she some rich bitch, stuck-up actress? Hmm. Maybe not.

"I shouldn't leave the camera station unattended too long, but if there's an extra cup, I'd be very grateful," he told her.

"How do you take it? Cream or sugar? Lemon or honey?"

she asked.

"Nothing. Just plain." He wasn't a complicated guy. At least not with his choice in tea.

She waved him on, giving him a gentle smile. "You go back, and I'll bring it out to you."

"Much obliged," he said, surprised as the old-fashioned words came out of his mouth. Was he a cowboy in some bad Western now? Who said that anymore? *Argh.*

He made his escape, going back to the foyer and sitting down. There were two chairs in the station. During the day, there were two guards on duty. One to watch the cameras and one to deal with anything that might come up. At night, there was just Nick inside the house and a whole lot of technology set up in strategic places around the perimeter.

He checked the monitors and status lights. Nothing was moving outside, or in the public areas of the house, for that matter. Miss Lane had drawn the line at having her private rooms set up with cameras, but she had panic buttons and sound sensors that would alert to any loud noise, which was the next best thing.

Of course, with a jaguar shifter on duty in the quiet of the night, he'd probably hear anything happening in the house long before a sensor would detect it. Like right now. He heard her slippers making little shuffling noises as she walked down the marble tiled hall toward him. His sensitive nose had picked up the scent of hot tea wafting toward him from the kitchen long ago and now mixed that aroma with the delicate scent of Sullivan's skin and the light floral shampoo she favored.

It was a delicious combination that made it hard for Nick to concentrate on his mission, but he was a professional. He'd manage. Somehow.

"Here you go," Sullivan said as she approached.

He noticed she had two steaming mugs in her hands, walking carefully so as not to spill any of the contents. She held one out to him, which he took in his much larger hands, the contrast between her delicate bone structure and his big paws making an emphatic statement in his mind about the differences between them.

He thanked her as he stood to take the mug, and then, she surprised him by hooking one slipper-shod foot around the leg of the empty chair and drawing it closer. She sat down with him, behind the little desk of the security station, and smiled as if having tea in the middle of the night with a stranger she'd hired to protect her was perfectly normal.

Nick sat back down, leaving as much space as he could between them within the tight confines of the desk area. They both had to rest their hot mugs on the desk, after all, so they needed to squeeze in to be within reach. Plus, he didn't want her to think he was shying away from her. On the contrary, it was hard to hold a distance with his inner cat wanting to rub right up against her so badly.

What had gotten into him? He'd been around beautiful women before, and none had ever affected his inner beast so much. Although, to be honest, Sullivan wasn't a classic beauty. She had a sharper edge to her than the porcelain-skinned dolls or darkly curvaceous beauties currently in favor in Hollywood. She had a style all her own that was both striking and nontraditional.

It was her acting ability that had driven her to stardom. Nick had taken time to see her new movie—as well as a few of her older films. He counted it as research but had found himself staring at Sullivan Lane up on the screen for reasons he couldn't quite define. She intrigued him on every level, and he was hoping like hell that she wasn't going to turn out to be a rat looking to make an even bigger name for herself by outing shifters to some tabloid.

If she had the proof they feared, she could very well screw up the shifter world with her revelation. No group of shifters wanted to be the one to open that particular can of worms. If the humans did find out, Nick was determined that it wasn't going to be because of a silly jaguar kid taking a fright. How ignominious.

"So, what do you think of the night shift so far, Nick? I

can call you Nick, right?" Her smile was as enchanting in person as it was on the silver screen.

He nodded. "It's been pretty standard, so far, until you showed up with the tea. Thank you, again, by the way. I'm not a coffee man, so tea is actually perfect for me," he told her, trying his best to be non-threatening.

His Alpha's new mate had been calling him Attila the Bodyguard lately, and he didn't necessarily like it. She had other names for him, too, which weren't exactly complimentary. Of course, they'd met under trying circumstances when he'd been interrogating her about an attempt on his Alpha's life. Nick had seen her talking with the gunman before the shooting and justifiably suspected that she might have something to do with the assassination attempt.

He'd done his duty and grilled her for an hour or more before the Alpha had come back with the news that she hadn't been involved after all. He'd spent the hour doing his own investigation at the hotel, where she and the gunman had coincidentally both been staying, which revealed that not only was she innocent but also, very likely, his mate.

Nick had been as stunned as the rest of the Clan. Mark had searched the world over for his one true mate and had never even come close to finding her. Then, all of a sudden, like lightning, there she was. It had taken a bit of getting used to, but Nick was beginning to like the new Alpha female of the Clan. She had good ideas for the new community they were building and seemed to have her heart in the right place.

There was no forgetting the fact that they had gotten off on the wrong foot. She still wasn't all that friendly toward him, but he hoped, someday, she'd realize that he'd only been such a hard ass because the safety of his Alpha came first. He hoped, in time, she'd forgive him for being so rough on her. That day hadn't quite come yet, though.

"A man who likes tea, who isn't British. Cool. I feel like I just discovered pirate treasure. You're a rarity, my friend." She raised her mug in joking salute before taking another sip. "You're not British, right?" she asked after, her brows drawing together in question.

"I don't think so," he replied. "My family hails from various parts of South America, but the States are my home for now."

"All of them? Or just California?" she teased, a very attractive joyful light shining in her eyes.

"California is the most recent, but I spend a lot of time in New York, too." He kept his answers deliberately vague.

"An international man of mystery," she mused. "I like that."

They sat in silence for a few moments, each enjoying their tea. It wasn't an uncomfortable silence, Nick found. Just two souls sharing the quiet of the night. There were hidden depths to Sullivan Lane, he was discovering.

"To answer your question, the night shift suits me just fine," he said some moments later, hoping to draw her out a bit more. Who knew when he'd have another chance to talk to her like this? He had to develop a feel for her personality in order to gauge how much of a threat she was to his people. Best to not waste any opportunities. "I'm nocturnal by nature, I guess." An old master at subterfuge, Nick knew just the right amount of truth to add to his words.

"You're a night owl, huh?" she asked with a slight grin.

"Something like that," he agreed. Though he had fur, not feathers.

"I've worked nights, so I know what you mean. There's a different energy to the world at night. Sort of crystalline and delicate, yet powerful. I always enjoyed the drive home at four in the morning when almost everyone else was asleep and there was nothing but me and the stars to light my path."

Hidden depths, indeed.

CHAPTER 2

"What did you do that kept you out at such dangerous hours?" he asked gently, wanting to know more but not wanting to push too hard.

"I was on the cleaning staff at a theater where they had bands and traveling companies come through all the time. The shows would end around ten or eleven at night, then the guys from the stage hands union would go in and break down the sets or instruments or whatever and then give our cleaning crew the go ahead to clean the seating areas and backstage. We always started with the lobby, restrooms and public areas, but we couldn't go into the theater and finish the seating and performing areas until they had cleared out enough of their equipment to make the place safe for us, so we were always the last ones out."

Sullivan Lane had been a cleaning lady? Nick found admiration starting to grow for the woman who didn't seem to shy away from hard work. Maybe she wasn't a rich bitch, stuck-up starlet, after all? He had to revise his opinion. He'd had her pegged all wrong, which wasn't a comfortable thing to admit, even in the privacy of his own mind.

"Is that where you caught the acting bug?" he asked, wanting to know more about this new facet of Sullivan Lane that he'd just uncovered.

"I don't know. Maybe. We didn't really get to see the shows. By the time we came in for work, they were nearly over, and we weren't allowed in the theater until after the crowds left, but every once in a while, they'd leave a door open to the lobby and I could just see in a little. I enjoyed the plays—what I could see of them. The musicals were nice, too, but I can't carry a tune in a bucket." She chuckled lightly, an inviting sound that begged him to join in. "To be honest, I never had dreams of all this." She gestured to the grand foyer and the big house all around them. "I wasn't one of those actresses who had a side gig as a waitress. I was just a waitress who had a side gig as an actress. All the films I've been in started out as poorly funded indie projects. This last one just took off in ways nobody expected because of the director, Raja Kapoor. He's kind of a genius."

Whether or not the young Indian director who'd successfully made the jump from Bollywood to Hollywood was really a genius or just a guy who could spot amazing talent remained to be seen. What was not in dispute in Nick's mind was Sullivan's incredible portrayal of a real-life heroine. She'd been spectacular and had some gripping scenes that were written by another up-and-comer, a screenwriter chosen by Kapoor. The team of nascent talent the young director had put together for this film was what had driven its success, at least in Nick's mind.

But he was hearing something in Sullivan's words and tone. She wasn't entirely happy with the way things had turned out. Surprising.

"Is this one of those cases of *be careful what you wish for*?" he asked gently.

"That's just it," she said, meeting his gaze directly. "I didn't wish for any of this. I was doing okay as a waitress, and I certainly wasn't getting death threats or bloody dead squirrels on my front steps. I also didn't need a bodyguard just to go to the grocery store." She huffed out a breath and calmed. "I'm sorry. I must sound like the most ungrateful wretch to you."

"Not at all. You've had an upheaval in your life, coupled with threats nobody would take lightly. You're entitled to wish it all away for a moment…as long as you realize you can't, in the end. Which is why you did the sensible thing and hired us to look out for you. Your circumstances have changed, and you can't stuff that genie back in the bottle. You're Sullivan Lane, and you're going to have to adapt to your new circumstances."

She gave him a sidelong look. "Harsh, but true." She shook her head. "And there are benefits to this change in my circumstances, as you put it. Having money is nice. Not having to worry about scrimping and saving and holding down a steady job for the first time in my life is kind of liberating," she admitted. "And the house is gorgeous, even if it isn't mine to keep. Eventually, when the heat dies down a bit, I want to buy a nice little place of my own—not something this gaudy or big, but something I can turn into a real cozy home. With all due consideration for security, of course." She nodded to him respectfully. "And please, call me Sal. We might as well be on a first-name basis since it's the middle of the night and I'm drinking tea with you in my pajamas."

Nick did chuckle, then, enjoying her sense of humor. "How did you get Sal from Sullivan?"

"It's the other way around. My name was always Sal. Sullivan is a stage name. The tabloids shortened it to Sully, which I'm not crazy about, but I haven't tried correcting them," she said offhandedly.

"All right, Sal, then" he said agreeably. "I had you pegged all wrong, and I'm sorry to admit I thought you might be like a lot of other Hollywood starlets."

Her eyes narrowed a little, but she didn't seem to take offense. "Spoiled rotten, you mean?" She laughed outright. "Don't worry. I don't have any delusions of grandeur. I'm probably a flash in the pan, and after this movie, I just might be able to go back into obscurity."

"Oh, I seriously doubt that," he told her. "I've seen the

movie, you know. It was part of my prep for taking on this job. You've got real talent. A presence that sort of steps off the screen and into your head," he told her, inadvertently revealing more than he'd intended, but he supposed it was okay. It was the middle of the night, after all, when secrets were more easily shared. "I don't think Hollywood is going to leave you alone. Offers are probably already rolling in, aren't they?"

She looked a bit guilty. "Yeah." She sighed. "My agent says I can have my pick of projects, which is really kind of amazing, but I guess it hasn't all sunk in yet. This business with the death threats has sort of taken the shine off this experience for me, you know?"

Suddenly, Nick wanted to bash the stalker's face in. How dare some unknown perv ruin what should be Sal's moment of triumph?

"I can see how that would put a damper on your enthusiasm, but you've done the right thing here, calling us in. We can protect you and hopefully give you the peace of mind to be able to enjoy your success the way you should."

She raised her mug in silent toast to his words and drained the rest of the tea. She stood, then, and he realized he was sorry to see this intimate moment out of time come to an end.

"Well, I'd better try to get back to sleep. I've got an appearance tomorrow with the rest of the cast. We're doing a charity thing that should be fun, and useful, too. We're raising funds for the local hospital, which I think is a good cause. Somebody actually paid ten grand to have lunch with me. Can you believe it?"

"I believe it," Nick answered without hesitation.

She shook her head, smiling as if she couldn't understand what motivated some people, then turned to walk away. But she paused, just a few steps away, turning back to look at him.

"Thanks for what you said about my work," she said, almost shyly. "It means a lot."

Nick saw in that moment that Sal Lane was a creature of delicate sensibilities. She might present a tough exterior to the world, but deep down she was just another fragile human soul, seeking friendship and approval. He could give her that, at the very least.

"I meant every word, Sal," he told her in a soft voice meant to convey compassion and belief.

She held his gaze for a moment longer then nodded slightly, just once, and turned to go. He watched her walk toward the stairs. There was more he wanted to say, but now was not the time. Maybe that time would never come. He just wasn't sure.

There was something so compelling about her, yet she confused him. It was like there were two Sullivan Lanes inside her—the one she presented to the world, and one that she protected, hiding that special light from everybody. Until he cleared up the mystery surrounding this woman, he wouldn't fully understand what she was to him.

For the more he was around her, the more he became convinced that she was significant to his future in some way. But his inner cat was puzzled. On the one hand, her scent was so familiar. So compelling. On the other, her words and deeds were secretive in a way the jaguar couldn't understand. There was something about her—some hidden depth that he needed to understand before he would know what she was to him.

Friend or enemy. Acquaintance or…mate?

Sweet Mother of All. Could he have really have just shared a late-night cup of tea with his future mate?

It didn't seem possible. Usually, jaguars knew their mates the moment they first scented them. Of course, it didn't *always* happen like that, but nine times out of ten, scent was what alerted them to their perfect matches.

The fact that Sal was human, and an actress, might have something to do with the disorder of his senses. He knew she smelled of something…beautiful…but he had no frame of reference. He wasn't sure what his nose was telling him, and the uncertainty annoyed his inner cat.

To be sure, it enjoyed puzzles, but this was getting a little ridiculous. The jaguar was on a mission, and the confusion wasn't helping. In fact, it was hindering his investigation and confounding his instincts. Not good. Not good at all.

Was she doing it on purpose? Did she have some way of hampering his senses? Was she in league with evil to have such a weapon against him? Or was it all just circumstantial? He had no idea, but he redoubled his resolve to keep his eyes open on this case. There could be a whole lot more going on here than he first realized.

*

Nick searched every nook and cranny of the rented house over the next few days, finding nothing. He went through all the papers she had in her study—mostly bills and scripts. He found that she'd been telling the truth about her career as a waitress. Last year's tax return listed a small restaurant in the next county as her employer. Previous returns had listed her on staff at a cleaning service, as well.

He also ran her social security number and learned that she had started out life with a different name. That wasn't altogether surprising since she was an actress and stage names were the norm. Sullivan Lane had started life as Sally Lannier, but she hadn't used that name in more than a few years except on a few legal documents, like her taxes.

Nick discovered that she was meticulous in her bookkeeping, balancing everything to the penny. He liked that. Order was important to him, as well. And she wasn't a spendthrift. She had carefully budgeted for all of her expenditures. He found her notes and the raw numbers she'd been working with. It sure looked like she was carefully squirreling away most of her money.

That ran counter to what he'd thought most young starlets who suddenly became rich and famous might do. He'd expected extravagant expenditures. Instead, she'd bought a new car—a practical vehicle, not anything ostentatious with a high price tag and a fancy name. No, she'd opted for something that would last for years, if she wanted to keep it that long. Time would tell.

As Nick worked his way through her personal stuff, he built a picture in his mind of a woman very unlike his expectations. She was a saver. Careful with her money and how she spent it. She didn't scrimp on necessary things, but she seemed aware that her windfall was new and fragile.

Not that he thought her career was over after only one hit movie. It could be, but he thought she had a lot of talent, if she wanted to keep on acting. What impressed him was that she wasn't counting on future income. No, she was hoarding her winnings while she had them...just in case.

Cautious. Practical. Talented and not full of herself. She appealed to his own no nonsense nature. It would have been so easy for someone in her position to go hog wild, buying all sorts of crazy stuff, but she hadn't. That spoke well of her personal control and maturity, and impressed the hell out of him.

As part of her security team, he had access to her daily schedule. So far, he hadn't seen any suspicious activity as far as meetings with the press went. There were no clandestine assignations with reporters from the tabloids. All of her press appointments had neat little agendas attached about what they planned to cover in each interview or appearance—all having to do with the recent movie as far as Nick had seen.

What he really needed to check out was her cell phone, but she kept the darn thing with her at all times. At night, it charged on her bedside table. He'd noted the cord placed oh-so-conveniently there on the nightstand when he'd done a security sweep of every room early on. There hadn't been any time where she wasn't with the phone long enough for him to get in and either crack its encryption or make a clone of the files on it for him to sift through later.

He had all the equipment and skills needed to do it, he just lacked the opportunity.

Disappointingly, there had been no more late-night tea tastings. She had been keeping a tight schedule of interviews and publicity appearances, the PR folks making the most of the unexpected hit they had on their hands. As a result, she was tired when she finally returned home each night, and by the time Nick came on duty, she was already fast asleep, and stayed that way all night.

Nick worked the midnight-to-seven shift in the house, so he didn't often cross paths with her. During the day, he shadowed her schedule—sometimes officially, filling in gaps in the security team as she went to and fro her various appointments, and sometimes unofficially, being a face in the crowd, using all his stealth skills to keep an eye on her from a short distance. Mostly, he listened, ready to spring into action the moment she said anything the least damaging about his people or any evidence she might have pertaining to shapeshifters.

He'd been doing that for a week, now, and frankly, he didn't think she was going to spill the beans, if she actually had them. He thought, if she did have video, she would have shown it to someone by now, but that didn't mean his assignment here was over. He was the head of security for the entire jaguar Clan. He decided when this mission was complete, and so far, he wasn't satisfied. Not by a long shot.

Whether that decision was made by his head or by something a little lower down, he wasn't entirely sure, but the inner jungle cat was demanding he stay and watch over the woman. His instincts were to keep her safe, and he'd learned long ago not to argue with them.

Especially since he'd intercepted another decapitated squirrel at the front gate to the mansion when he'd gone on duty last night. The nut job who had threatened her before was at it again, and he'd found her new home. Not good.

All of Nick's protective instincts rose to an angry bristle. Her manager had decided not to tell Sal about the new threat just yet after Nick had called his chain of command at the security company and reported the near-breach. Personally, he thought that was the wrong call, but technically, he wasn't in charge of this operation.

His buddies who owned the security company probably realized Nick had a hidden agenda, but they trusted him enough to let it play out. He was on the team as a special favor, and they knew he wouldn't do anything that might damage their business or reputation. There was a long history between them all, and none of them would betray the other in any way.

Of course, the guys who owned Halibut Security were all former Navy SEALs. The somewhat fishy name of their company was a bit of a joke between them. It was also a combo of their last names. Haffern, Linelli and Buttons were the three principle owners, and all were human.

Nick wasn't sure if they realized that many of their friends and work associates from the Teams were shifters. Oh, they might understand that some guys had special skills, but they probably didn't understand exactly where they came from. It was a well-hidden fact that a bunch of selkies had created the Navy SEAL program in the Viet Nam era, and many other kinds of shifters had gone out for the Teams ever since.

There were quite a few humans who made the cut as well, and if their teammates had a little extra instinct, or strength, or whatever, nobody commented openly. There was a code they all followed, and they were brothers in arms, regardless of their exact species.

It helped that the admiral in charge of all Special Operators was himself, a creature of myth and magic. He knew how to best utilize the special talents of each group he put together, and he had created a few very selective shifter-only squads that he used in cases where humans would never discover exactly how they accomplished their near-impossible tasks.

In this operation, Nick was the only shifter on the team. He reported directly to Linelli, a guy he'd worked with a few times during his stint in the Special Forces. They'd always had a good working relationship, and that seemed to carry through to civilian life, as well. Nick had called in the discovery of the dead rodent just after midnight, and Linelli had dispatched extra guys to work the perimeter overnight.

There hadn't been any additional problems, and the decision on what to do about the threat had been put off until the morning. Nick had asked for and been given a double shift, following Sal at a discreet distance as she went about her public relations appearances during the day. He'd caught a few hours of sleep while she attended a gala fundraising dinner and was ready for duty again that night.

By that time, her handlers had decided not to tell her about the renewed threat. Nick thought that was a bad call. It was her life on the line. She deserved to know. But he had to keep reminding himself—he wasn't in charge here.

Still, his instincts clamored for him to get additional personnel on the ground. Which was why he placed another call to Linelli just after midnight.

"I know you guys specialize in security," Nick said, trying to be diplomatic, which wasn't really his strong suit. "But what about investigations?"

"We generally leave that to the police," Linelli admitted. "We're strictly bodyguards and security systems."

"What if I could get you an investigator I've worked with before? A guy with our kind of experience and a boatload of discretion?" Nick really wanted to get to the bottom of the threat to Sal's safety. Just guarding her against danger wasn't enough. He wanted the danger eradicated completely. Killed. Dead.

"I don't know. It's not something we really do... But, if you feel that strongly about it..."

"I do," Nick told him when Linelli trailed off. "Something really bad is going down here, friend. You know my instincts are never wrong. Think what it would do to your company's reputation if you lost her to violence."

"Shit." Linelli sighed heavily over the phone line. "You really believe that, don't you?"

"I *fear* it," Nick admitted quietly. Guys like them didn't

often admit to fear.

There was silence for a moment on the other end of the line, then Linelli spoke again. "Who do you have in mind?"

"Ever hear of a guy named Collin Hastings?"

"Hear of him? Hell, man. He's like the most exclusive private investigator in the country. Everybody wants to hire him, but nobody can get past his screening process. He only takes on very special cases, from what I hear."

"I can get him. Guaranteed." Nick might be stretching the truth a little bit, but he didn't doubt that, if Hastings wouldn't come running at his call, he could ask his Alpha to make a special request that could not be refused. At least, not lightly.

"Shit, Nick. You've got more surprises in you than a Mini full of clowns." Nick could hear the respectful exasperation in Linelli's voice. "Okay. Call him. If you can get that guy, I know discretion is a given. We don't want this getting around, but you're right, it would be a complete disaster if we lost a client to a fruitcake that gets his jollies killing squirrels and scaring ladies." Linelli paused, then continued, "I'll talk to Buttons and Haffern. You talk only to your contact. Nobody else. I don't want the rest of the security team knowing that we're going outside our bailiwick on this one. The investigation is your baby. You interface with Hastings and report back directly to me. We need to keep this quiet, but I also want to know what's going on, so regular reports would be appreciated."

Nick knew that meant they were *mandatory*, but he had expected that. It was Linelli's company's reputation on line, after all.

"Roger that," Nick replied. "I'll call him and let you know once he's accepted the case."

Linelli chuckled. "You're that sure of yourself. Man, you've got brass ones, Nick. Glad you're on our side."

They hung up after exchanging a few more words, and Nick got right to work, contacting the premier shifter detective in the United States. He had a big favor to ask.

CHAPTER 3

Hastings agreed to come up to Hollywood from his current base of operations in Las Vegas the next day, but as it turned out, that wasn't soon enough. In the middle of the night, the silent alarms started going off, one after another. The perimeter was being breached in a big way.

Nick tried to mobilize the perimeter guards, but nobody was responding to his radio calls. Shit was happening, and he had only one thought—protect Sal at all costs. He couldn't do that effectively from the marble foyer. No, he had to have eyes on her.

Nick took the steps up to the second floor four at a time, making light work of climbing the sweeping staircase that led to the bedrooms. He followed the scent of fear to Sal's bedroom, his heart climbing into his throat at the silent indicator that she knew something was very wrong.

He smelled something else, as well...a predatory scent. Pungent. Sickly sweet. Madness. Obsession. Shifter.

Oh, shit. Sal's stalker was a crazy-assed shifter. It wasn't common, but sometimes, shifters did lose touch with reality and go bat-shit crazy. He hadn't encountered that scent often, but he recognized it now. The bastard was up here. Close to Sal. Or had been. The scent was growing fainter...

Nick burst into Sal's bedroom to find her holding a

handgun with an expert grip. The sliding glass door that led to a small balcony was wide open, filmy curtains blowing in the night breeze. The shifter was gone.

The scent trail went out that way and down. He'd jumped, Nick saw right away, going to the balcony, discounting the fact that Sal still held her handgun. She wouldn't shoot him. And if she did—unless she'd loaded her pea shooter with silver bullets—he'd heal. The risk was negligible.

Nick wanted desperately to follow the mad shifter's trail, but he had conflicting desires. On the one hand, he wanted to hunt. On the other, he wanted to protect. He couldn't exactly jump off the balcony in Sal's sight. That would raise more questions than he was prepared to answer. And he couldn't leave her alone. Not when the perimeter team still wasn't answering their radios.

He very much feared they'd been taken out by the shifter. It wouldn't have been too difficult. A crazed shifter, uncaring about secrecy, could easily have used his superior strength and senses to take down a group of human security guards in quick succession, leaving his path to his target clear.

Nick wanted to growl, thinking of Sal as a *target*. That just wasn't right. She was a caring, beautiful woman. Not a target.

He closed and locked the balcony door, for all the good it would do. Then, he turned back to her, glad to note she had lowered her handgun but kept it ready at her side.

"Let's get you out of here," he said in as calm a tone as he could manage. He picked up the slinky robe lying across the chest at the foot of her bed and handed it to her.

She put it on, never relinquishing her handgun. Good girl. He liked her instincts. She wasn't going to be one of those silly girls in the horror movies who hide in the basement or give the bad guy their only weapon. No, Sal was a fighter. Nick's inner cat liked that. A lot.

"How did he get past the guards outside?" she asked as she joined him near the door to her bedroom. She wasn't balking at coming with him, and her question was a good one.

"That's what I need to find out, but first, I need to keep you safe. This room is too exposed, and I need to get to the com equipment, though help should already be on its way with how many alarms were going off as I ran up the stairs." He started out the door with her close behind, his senses stretched to their maximum range, just in case the bad guy had only been bluffing about running away. "Stick close to me," Nick told her. "Unless we run into trouble, then hug a wall and give me room to fight, but stay in sight so I know you're okay. Clear?"

"Clear," she replied, as if she was one of his men, acknowledging orders.

He heard her gulp and knew she wasn't as calm about all this as she was pretending to be, but he'd take it. She was holding up well so far, which made his job a whole lot easier. He knew from past experience that it was really difficult to protect someone who didn't know how to listen and follow orders. And she was armed. He hadn't realized she had a handgun, which was something she should have told Halibut about when she hired them, but he wasn't too upset about it.

"You know how to handle that thing?" he asked, nodding toward the weapon still held in her right hand, pointed toward the ground.

She nodded. "I haven't always been as you see me now. I learned how to defend myself when I was very young, and I keep in practice. I hit what I aim at."

Better and better. Nick's inner jaguar wanted to purr. His mate was hell on wheels when faced with danger.

Wait a minute. Mate?

Nick paused and would have swayed if he wasn't holding onto the banister at the top of the stairs. Crap. He'd gone and done it. He'd found his mate. The cat had known but had, for some unknown reason, waited to spring it on his human half until just this minute. Great. Just great.

Nick went down the stairs—one at a time on this trip—with Sal following close behind. He let his senses guide him. No threats down here that he could discern. He led her to the security desk in the front foyer and parked her in the spare chair while he plugged into the system and made the necessary calls.

"What's going on over there?" Linelli asked when Nick got him on the line. "Judging by my remote alarms, all hell is breaking loose." Some of the sensors were mirrored to a second panel that Linelli, or any of the principles of Halibut Security, could access at any time to check on both their clients and their employees.

Nick gave a concise sitrep, filling his old friend in on the situation. "I've got the client with me," he told Linelli first. "I haven't been able to check on the guys stationed outside."

"No worries. Keeping the client safe is your first priority." As Nick had known, but it was good to hear Linelli taking Sal's safety as seriously as Nick did. "Backup should be to you within the next three to four minutes. I'll check on their ETA. I'll coordinate from here for the moment, but will come down if the client wants someone to yell at."

Nick almost laughed at the resignation in Linelli's tone. Apparently, working with the Hollywood elite created situations where he had to be the designated stooge. Better him than me, Nick thought. He would *not* have enjoyed having to listen to some *civilian* harangue him about how to do his job.

"The lady is cool under fire," Nick was glad to report. "And armed."

"No shit?" Linelli sounded impressed. "Does she know what she's doing?"

"Looks like it," Nick reported.

"I knew I liked her when she signed up." For Linelli, that was high praise, indeed. "You should see the first squad arrive. They're coming in openly. Black SUV. They'll blink their lights for you. The second, third, and fourth units will come in on foot, on the flanks and from behind. They'll check on the original team and report back directly to me. I'll let you know what we find out."

"I expect you'll find everyone incapacitated. Probably

knocked out by blows to the head. At best, you're going to have some concussions to deal with," Nick said, knowing his tone was grim. He might have to get creative in how he reported this to Linelli.

Though the human ex-SEAL might suspect there was something a little larger-than-life to some of his former co-workers, the secret wasn't out. There was a don't-ask, don't-tell policy pertaining to shifters in the armed forces. Nick wouldn't be the one to reveal the secret—even to someone as cool as Linelli. This entire mission was all about preserving the shifter secret.

"A team, then? More than one perpetrator?" Linelli was on alert again.

"No. Only one," Nick said. "We're secure for now. Perp's gone."

"What kind of man could get all of them?" Linelli asked the million-dollar question, of course. He was no slouch.

"I've run into something like this before," Nick told his old friend, skirting the question. "Most of it is still compartmentalized, but I can say, it's possible. I recognize the mode of attack."

Linelli gave a long-suffering sigh. "And here I thought I left all that secret super power shit behind when I left the Teams." Linelli muttered a few curses before continuing. "All right. If you're right, most of the team is going to be out for a few weeks nursing concussions. Since it sounds like you have the top-secret decoder ring—which nobody ever saw fit to give me—I'll let you run with this. I assume you have men in mind to reconstitute the night shift?"

Nick wasn't imagining the edge in Linelli's voice. The human knew darn well that there were certain secrets kept even from fellow Special Operators, and he sounded more than a little bitter about his lack of knowledge. Nick understood. He couldn't help illuminate things in this case, but he definitely understood. It was frustrating to run a mission with bad or missing intel.

"Hastings arrives later today. Some of his folks would be

perfect for this job."

Another one of those annoyed sighs. "Okay. Pick your team. Send them to me, and I'll sign off on them once they clear background checks. There are liability issues since Miss Lane's contract is with Halibut, but if we put Hastings' people on as sub-contractors or something, we should be able to do this. I'll sort it out. For now, just keep her safe. Make contact with the backup teams and report back in thirty. Linelli out."

Nick had to chuckle. Sounded like Linelli forgot he was talking on a phone and not a tactical radio. The line went dead as Linelli hung up without further ado, which was just as well. Nick had things to do on his end, and Sal was still sitting next to him, looking stunned but determined.

"Backup is here," he told her. "I just need to talk to them, and then, we can decide what you want to do for the rest of tonight."

"I don't want to stay here," she said almost immediately.

"All right," Nick replied slowly. He hadn't really thought about where he could stash her for the night, but he'd figure something out. First, though, he had to interface with the squads that were securing the perimeter. "You okay here with me?" he asked her gently as he saw the big black SUV roll into the driveway and flick its lights in the prearranged pattern.

"Yeah. I'm sticking to you like glue for now, Nick. Sorry." She swallowed hard, her body trembling just the slightest bit.

"Don't be sorry. That's what I'm here for. To keep you safe. Stick with me, kid, and you'll be fine. I promise." He made that vow even as he raised the short-range radio they used on site and made contact with the men in the SUV, giving them the proper code before they piled out of the dark vehicle.

Nick pushed the button that would unlock the front door for them. A minute later, seven big guys entered in the foyer then fanned out to search the rest of the house. The team leader—a behemoth named Doug—stayed in the foyer with Nick and Sal, communicating with his guys on their own radio frequency and reporting their progress back to Nick, who was site commander in this situation.

The house was clear, which was no surprise to Nick. The scent of insane shifter had faded. The perp was long gone. At least for tonight. Now, Nick just had to figure out where to take Sal for what remained of the night.

"Let's go upstairs, and you can get dressed and pack an overnight bag," Nick said to her in a gentle voice.

"Where will we go?" He liked that she had no doubt he'd be by her side throughout. The cat wanted to purr in satisfaction. She was already seeing them as a couple.

"Not sure yet. Worst-case scenario, you can come back to my place. I have a spare room." It was a furnished rental he'd selected when he'd arrived in town. Secure building. Difficult approaches should anyone come for him for whatever reason. The guest room was full of equipment at the moment, but it wouldn't take long to clear off the twin bed in there for her use. "It's not the Ritz, but you'll be safe there for a few hours until we decide what we're going to do about tonight's events."

"Let's just do that," she said quietly. "I'm still a little too shaky to make good decisions right now. If I can stay with you, I think I'll be able to calm down and think clearly. I'm sorry to invade your personal space, though. Are you sure it's all right?"

"I'm sure," he told her as he escorted her up the stairs. He went into her bedroom and checked both it and the attached bathroom while she watched. The place was empty. "You can change in the bathroom. I'll be right out here, securing the sliding door and looking for clues."

He flashed her what he hoped was a reassuring grin and was glad to see the corners of her mouth curve upward slightly as she went to her dresser and pulled out a few items of clothing. He tried not to notice the silky underwear in her hand. He really did.

Nick turned away, willing his raging attraction to settle down. The last thing he wanted to do was scare her off.

Luckily, the radio drew his attention as she walked into the bathroom, the other teams reporting in. As Nick had suspected, the original guards were down with blows to the head. Thankfully, it wasn't worse. That shifter could have just as easily killed them all.

Then, his cell phone rang. It was Linelli, calling earlier than expected.

"Problems?" Nick asked by way of greeting.

"Fucking concussions, man. In the Teams, if someone rang your bell, you just shook it off and kept going. In civilian life, it means a shitload of paperwork and medical testing, plus time off work. Your original team is toast, Nick. They're all going to be at the ER for the next few hours, then off duty until the damage can be fully assessed."

"I figured. I'm just glad they're not dead," he replied honestly.

"Yeah, there is that," Linelli agreed in a somber tone. "Anything that could blow through five guys that efficiently could have done a lot worse." He paused. "You recognize this?"

"Yeah," Nick admitted, saying nothing more. Linelli had to have run up against this sort of thing when he was in the Teams. He was a good man, but the shifter secret wasn't something Nick could share.

"I wish to hell I knew what you know," Linelli said at last, and Nick breathed a sigh of relief. Linelli had accepted the need for secrecy.

"Actually, I truly believe you wouldn't want the burden of this knowledge," Nick answered after a moment's thought. Linelli and the other human Special Operators thought of themselves as invincible. As the top of the food chain. The predators who protected the innocent.

They were all that, but if they knew about the existence of shifters among them, Nick honestly didn't think it would be good for morale. Sure, there were always some guys who were better at certain things than others, but in the end, they were united because they were all the same. Dedicated people who wanted to serve and protect with the special skills they had acquired through hard work, perseverance and training all the time.

If human Spec Ops soldiers suddenly became aware that the guys next to them weren't fully human, after all, it could cause a rift that might never be healed. All in all, Nick thought it was safer all around—for the humans and for shifters—to keep the existence of their kind under wraps. Possibly forever.

"I'll have to trust you on that," Linelli replied, and Nick felt a bit of satisfaction. Trust. That's what bonded them. Linelli trusted Nick and was willing to put his business on the line and allow Nick to keep his secrets in order to protect their client. That meant a lot.

"I'm glad you do," Nick said honestly, hoping Linelli understood the very real emotion behind his words.

"What are you going to do with the client?" Linelli changed the subject neatly.

Of course, the question was a loaded one. There were *many* things Nick wanted to do with her. Most of them X-rated. But Linelli wanted to know about her security, so Nick got his mind out of the gutter and back on business. Admittedly, with some difficulty.

"She doesn't want to stay here," Nick told Linelli.

"Well, I can't say I blame her." Linelli paused, sighing audibly. "I'll have to think about where we can put her."

"No need." Nick knew this next part would cause Linelli's eyebrow to rise. He was famous for that one-eyebrow Vulcan question look of his. "I'm taking her to my place."

Linelli whistled through his teeth, making a horrible screeching sound over the phone speaker. Nick winced. Sometimes, humans were hard on shifter ears.

"My, my. You do work fast, young Nicholas."

"It's not like that—"

"I didn't think she was your type." Linelli talked right over Nick's protestations, but Nick couldn't let that statement stand.

"A gorgeous gal who meets danger with a nine mil in her hand? You bet she's my type," Nick said with an easy grin. "But my place is the most secure I know on short notice."

"You've got a condo somewhere, right? Wait a minute..." Nick heard the tapping of a keyboard on the other end of the line as Linelli looked up Nick's information. "Oh. Wilson Towers. Yeah, that's a good complex. I've stashed clients there myself. Solid floor plan. Good construction. Easy to defend."

"That's why I picked it," Nick agreed amiably. "And it came furnished. It's not too bad, actually."

That was an understatement. The place was owned by a rich Chinese businessman who only used the place twice a year. The rest of the time, he rented it out on a monthly basis. Nick had taken it for the month, not knowing how long he would need to wrap things up. That the businessman was one of the rare panda shifters was known only to a few, but the vast majority of those who rented the condo were also shifters, since he advertised mostly in places other shifters would see the listing.

"All right. Hourly check-ins until the end of your shift. I should have something better lined up by then. Or, if she wants to go back..."

"She said she wanted some time to clear her head and think out her next move. I expect I'll be able to let you know what she wants to do in the morning. I have no problem keeping her at the condo until she's ready to leave." In fact, he'd be happy if she just stayed with him. Period. But it was a little too soon to be saying such things to her.

"Sounds like a plan. I'll set up an escort and some decoy vehicles for your ride."

"Appreciate it. We'll be ready to roll in about ten minutes," Nick told Linelli, then went through the details of the move.

They would take as few chances as possible getting the client from her rented mansion to Nick's rented condo. It was a complex maneuver, but this was something Halibut

Security specialized in. Getting their celebrity clients from place to place while ditching paparazzi was a specialty.

When Nick ended the call, he was aware that Sal had come out of the bathroom some time before. She'd heard a few things that might have surprised her, but he hadn't turned around, giving her time to pack her overnight bag in relative privacy. He was facing the sliding glass doors, though, so he could see a filmy reflection through the sheer curtains of her moving around from closet to dresser and back again.

He replaced his cell phone in the small holster attached to his belt and turned to face her. He hadn't been sure what to expect, but he certainly was surprised to see her grinning at him, her delicate brows raised in question.

"So, pistol-packin' mamas are your type, eh?"

Nick was at a loss for words. He could hear the wry amusement in her tone, and it made him feel lighter...happy that he'd been able to make her feel joy even momentarily on this dark night.

He moved toward her, walking right up to face her from only two feet away. He watched her reaction carefully, not wanting to scare her or throw her off in any way. She'd had enough upset for one night.

But then, she surprised him. She took a step forward. Toward him. Closer than they'd ever been to each other. Her gaze met his and held... And then...

Nick bent slowly. So slowly. Giving her time to escape if she wanted to, but she didn't move away. In fact, she moved forward, joining her lips to his in their first kiss.

The first of many, he prayed as he'd never prayed before.

CHAPTER 4

Sal couldn't quite believe she was kissing Nick the bodyguard, but yeah, she was. And she wasn't about to feel sorry for it. On the contrary, he'd been the leading man in her dreams for the past week. Ever since they'd shared that late-night cup of tea, she hadn't been able to get him out of her mind.

Even during the day, when he wasn't on duty, she thought about him almost constantly. She wondered what he was doing when he wasn't with her. She wondered what kind of music he enjoyed. And most of all, she wondered what kind of lover he would be.

Oh, yeah. This kiss told her a lot about that last, most vital question.

He was both tender and demanding as he stepped closer, bringing her body against his. His muscles were hard and unyielding, but at the same time, she knew he would let her go at the least indication. He might be bigger than her, but she was in control. He gave her that. He seemed to be doing all in his power to reassure her and let her know in silent, mysterious ways that he would never hurt her.

He was a protector to the core. She had guessed that about him from their first meeting. It was pretty obvious, of course, from his choice of profession, but there was something deeper to him. Something almost spiritual. Like he had a calling to protect those who were smaller, weaker and more vulnerable than himself.

These weren't things most people would be able to discern. Sal accepted her differences, for the most part. At least the ones she could live with. She'd always been a little different. Like her mother.

Only Sal had rejected the writhing magic in her soul that had tried so hard to take her over—as it had taken over her poor mother. Sal had put a lid on it and sealed it up tight. The magic was something she never wanted to let free. It was too chaotic. Too dangerous.

But the little instinctual things… They were harmless enough and something she couldn't really control. Those instincts had helped her many times. They'd helped her pick the right course of action. They'd helped her prepare for difficult times. Hell, tonight, that little voice in the back of her mind had told her to wake up and grab her gun. Just in time, as it turned out.

The *knowing* had helped her many times. And this time, in this man's strong arms, it told her many things—many confusing things that she didn't quite understand—about him. Most of all, it told her she wanted to know more.

Sal's lips tingled where they touched his. Little zings of magic that made her wonder if there wasn't something truly special about Nick. Her body grew warm where she pressed against him, small zaps of energy bouncing between them, making her arousal rise.

She was so totally lost in the kiss that she didn't even hear the knock on the doorframe to her bedroom the first time. Neither did Nick, apparently, which was why the person trying to get their attention repeated the action…maybe more than once. She couldn't be certain.

"Pardon the interruption." A strong male voice came from the doorway, and they sprang apart.

For her part, she knew she was reacting out of fear and surprise. She wasn't altogether sure why Nick let go of her as if she was on fire and he'd been burned. Her gaze narrowed, and her spine stiffened.

Nick could have happily killed Doug at that moment. Shot him dead, right then and there. Or better yet, Nick imagined strangling Doug with his bare hands.

Of course, he did neither.

"What's up, Doug?" Nick asked instead, placing himself between Sal and Doug, blocking his view of the lady. It wasn't much protection, but it was at least something to give her a moment to collect herself before facing the world—or, at least, damned Doug—again.

"Grounds have been cleared. Our guys are on their way to the hospital. Convoy's ready to move out whenever you are," Doug reported, barely concealing his interest in the scene he'd interrupted.

"Convoy?" Sal asked, coming up beside Nick.

He noticed she had her nine-millimeter handgun in a holster under her arm as she shrugged into a dark jacket. *Easy, boy.* The fact that she was packing heat and apparently knew her way around concealed weapons was making him even hotter than he'd been already. *Damn.*

"We'll start out together, but there are a couple of decoy cars and escort vehicles to make sure everybody gets where they're going without a tail," Nick explained.

"Of course, at this time of night, there aren't that many cars on the roads, so it'll be easier to spot anyone who tries to follow," Doug put in.

"You guys are the experts," Sal replied, zipping her jacket halfway.

Nick approved. The half-zip allowed her quick access if she needed to get to the gun strapped under her arm. It also guaranteed that her jacket wouldn't blow open in the night breeze and show the world that she was carrying.

"You got everything you need?" Nick asked her, turning to take the small overnight bag from her. He'd carry this himself, to be certain nobody messed with her stuff.

"Yeah, I'm used to traveling light." She gave him a grin

that felt like sunshine warming him from the inside out.

He hefted the bag and grinned back at her. "You're not kidding. Are you sure it's enough?"

She nodded. "Plenty. I've got two changes of clothes in there, just in case."

Nick shook his head, marveling at the small size of the bag for what she claimed was in there. Then, he shrugged. She knew what she was doing. So far tonight, she'd impressed him with her cool-headedness under fire, her familiarity with personal protection, and her willingness to listen to his advice. She also hadn't thrown the least little bit of a hissy fit at the idea of leaving this lap of luxury for a condo she'd never even seen.

They accomplished the move with little fuss. Linelli had set up the decoy operation, and his guys were the best in the business at this sort of thing. Nick was on the phone with Linelli or Doug almost constantly during the ride to his place, either reporting progress or getting reports from the other vehicles and teams involved. All went off without a hitch, and Nick breathed a sigh of relief as he entered the private underground parking area below the condo.

Two of Linelli's guys had been pre-positioned there—they had access because Halibut Security already had contacts in this condo complex and had the proper codes. They gave Nick the *all clear* before he opened the door to the SUV he'd been driving and went around to help Sal out.

She followed his lead, quiet and watchful as they made their way to the private elevator that led to the condo he was renting. In another setting, it might've been called a penthouse suite, but here, it was simply one-half of the top floor of this high-rise condo tower. Only residents of the two top floors got to use this particular elevator. There was a special key card involved, which Nick produced from his pocket as they neared the doors. He signaled to the two men who'd been watching the garage for the past twenty minutes to join him and Sal in the elevator.

Halibut might have access to the communal parking, but

they didn't have clearance for the exclusive express elevator. Normally, Nick would've handled checking the condo himself, but he had Sal to think of and Halibut procedures to follow. He had two trained men he knew by sight, so there was no question they weren't Halibut employees. Linelli had been careful who he'd called in to do this late-night extra duty.

Nick would play along and let the guys clear the condo before he brought Sal inside. It was procedure, he knew. It would make Linelli happy. And even though Nick would bet his last dime that the stalker wouldn't have figured out where they were going so quickly, it couldn't hurt to check things out.

"We'll just wait here a moment while they clear the rooms," he told her. It was the first moment they had alone when he wasn't on the phone since their kiss in her bedroom. He wasn't sure what to say to her, but he felt like he should say *something*.

"It's all right," she answered in a soft voice, and he wondered if she meant more than just the obvious with her words. Was she referring to their kiss and the awkwardness he felt now? Damn.

"Look..." He turned to talk to her, but at that exact moment, one of the guys stepped into view and waved them into the condo. Nick sighed heavily and ran a hand over the stubble on his jaw in frustration. He changed his mind about opening a can of worms in front of the troops and gestured for Sal to precede him. "After you, milady."

She gave him a quirky look that was almost a smile, but went ahead, into the condo. Nick closed the door behind himself, checking with the guys to see what they had to report. A quick hand signal told him what he'd suspected. The condo was clear.

Nick thanked the men on their way out then closed and locked the door behind them. Finally. He was alone with Sal. In his territory, temporary though it might be. It was still his for the duration of his stay here. He turned to watch her progress through the living room. There was so much he wanted to say to her, but he had to make sure she was okay with their kiss first.

"Sal…" he started, then his phone rang. For a moment, he fantasized about crushing the infernal device in his fist and flinging the little pieces against the wall, but he knew he couldn't do that. Taking a deep breath for calm, he lifted the phone from its holster on his belt and picked up the call.

It was Linelli, wanting a sit rep and final report before closing down the operation for the night. He went over the plans he'd made to station guards on the condo while she was there, but since there was only the express elevator or the emergency stairs to get to that floor, it was relatively easy to cover. Nick listened impatiently while Linelli went over the details, knowing it was necessary to maintaining his cover that he worked with the humans on this.

He answered the necessary questions and responded in the places he was expected to say something. He went into the kitchen area and got a couple of cold bottles of water out of the fridge, intending to bring one to Sal. He could just see her, sitting on the plush couch in the living room. The poor woman had been through a lot tonight. He talked quietly, giving her a moment of peace, to herself.

By the time he turned back to the living room, carrying the cold water bottles, she was fast asleep, curled into the corner of the wide sofa. He would have left her there, but her neck was resting at a funny angle that was sure to cause pain when she woke up. Coming to a decision on his next course of action, Nick went quietly into the spare bedroom and cleared it of his extra gear, turning down the bed and making it ready for her.

Then, he returned to the living room to find her still in that same uncomfortable-looking position. As gently as he could, Nick lifted her into his arms and walked down the hallway to the bedroom he'd prepared. When he lay her on the red silk sheets, in keeping with the Asian theme of the so-called Chrysanthemum Bedroom, he found it hard to let her go.

But he must. Sal was dead to the world. It wasn't fair to paw her while she was the next best thing to unconscious.

Feeling noble, Nick leaned close to place a chaste kiss on her forehead as he tucked her in. It was hard—scratch that, *he* was hard—but he left the room, pulling the door almost closed but leaving it enough ajar that some of the soft hallway illumination would spill into the room in case she should wake up and not recognize her surroundings. He didn't want her to be disoriented by darkness on top of being in a room she'd never seen before.

If she'd been a jaguar with superior night vision, he wouldn't have worried. Of course, if she'd been a jaguar, she wouldn't have been his mate. The Goddess knew he'd searched for years to find a mate among his own people, but after too many disappointments, he'd just about given up on ever finding the one female meant for him.

Until now. When he'd least expected it, there she was. A human, no less. He wasn't quite sure how to feel about that, but he was a great believer in the wisdom of the Mother of All. If the Goddess meant for him to be mated with a human, then who was he to question it?

Nick put in an early morning call to Collin Hastings, hoping the man would be able to move up their planned meeting. Sure enough, hearing of the escalation in the situation and the fact that a possibly feral shifter was involved, Hastings didn't wait for conventional transportation. Instead, he came by air.

In the darkness before dawn, a giant hawk—larger than any natural bird of prey—landed gently on the penthouse patio. Nick was waiting with a set of spare clothing—gym shorts, a new pair of socks and a sweatshirt—for the hawk shifter when he took his human form.

Nick left the folded clothing on the patio table with a nod to the giant hawk and went back inside, leaving the glass door open. They'd both been in the army. They were acquainted, but not close. Still, they had more in common than most, both being shifters trying to coexist with the human world. Even so, Nick gave the man a moment to gather himself and shift in private, just in case birds were ticklish about such things.

They might both be shifters, but cats and birds weren't natural buddies. Werehawks and jaguar shifters, though, had come to a sort of mutual respect over the years. This would be the first time they worked closely together, and Nick hoped to create better understanding between their two Clans. Nick knew his Alpha would appreciate strong allies like the raptors, if Nick could somehow gain that sort of trust between them. Time would tell.

Nick made breakfast while waiting for Hastings to come in from the balcony. He'd flown all the way, due to the urgency of the situation and the cooperative night-dark sky. He'd probably be hungry. The least Nick could do was feed the man.

Besides, it was close enough to dawn, and normal breakfast time, that Nick was feeling more than a bit peckish himself.

He heard the door to the balcony close and then the padding of sock feet across the plush carpet. Hawks weren't as stealthy in their human forms as the land-based predators, Nick had heard. Or maybe that was just an old wives' tale and Hastings was deliberately making noise that a shifter would pick up. Maybe he was just being polite. Who knew with bird shifters?

Regardless, Nick looked up to meet the other man's gaze. "Breakfast, Captain?"

"Thank you, Master Sergeant," Hastings said, taking the high seat at the kitchen island that Nick nodded toward.

"The last time our paths crossed," Nick said as he plated the mountain of pancakes, bacon and sausages he'd made for his guest, "we were both still in uniform."

"Fun times," Hastings replied, smiling fondly as Nick set one of the plates in front of him. "This looks great. Thanks.

I'm a little hungry after the long flight."

"Again, I appreciate your haste. I told you a bit about what happened last night, but I need to get the rest of the information to you before my guest wakes up." Nick could hear Sal's slow, even breathing. She was definitely still asleep, but that could change any time, and if she was around, they couldn't speak as freely.

"She in the guest room?" Hastings asked, shoveling a forkful of pancake into his mouth.

"Yeah. She practically passed out on the couch. I put her in the other room, but I don't know how long she'll sleep. So, we should probably get the sit rep out of the way first."

"Go," Hastings said, eating while listening attentively.

Nick filled him in on what he had seen, heard, and smelled the night before at the mansion. He also gave Hastings his impressions of the situation, including the file Linelli had put together that had police reports, photos and diagrams of the animal mutilation crimes.

"Nasty stuff," Hastings observed, looking at the photos of the decapitated squirrels. "Rodents are more my people's thing, but I guess some land-based shifters hunt them, too, right?"

"Wolves, foxes, some of the smaller cat breeds, and a few others, I guess," Nick replied. "I hadn't really thought about the perp being a flight shifter, though. That would cause a whole new set of problems."

"Which I can handle," Hastings was quick to say. "I wouldn't be happy hunting my own kind, but if he's gone over to the dark side, he's got to be put down, regardless."

Nick sighed and sat back, stuffing the gruesome photos back into the paper folder. He didn't want to leave them lying around, just in case Sal came out of the guest room.

"He didn't scent like a bird," Nick mused, placing the folder back in his laptop bag and digging into his own breakfast. "The scent was wild. Unwashed. Hard to place because of the stench, but I'd go with canine, if I had to pick a species. Wolf, probably. Or maybe fox...but I'd bet on wolf." Nick chewed thoughtfully for a moment. "Whatever he was, he didn't smell sane. Nobody lets themselves get that rank—and the worst odor was from his human side. I don't think he's shifted in a long time."

"Or maybe just to battle form and no further," Hastings commented, naming the in-between form where a shifter was still upright like a man, but with the animal's attributes. It was painful for shifters to hold the battle form, and only the strongest Alphas could manage it for any length of time. "Stopping the shift halfway every time—or getting stuck, for some reason—could drive the animal half-mad."

"Could it be some kind of magical attack on the perp? Someone made it so he couldn't complete the shift?" Nick asked, frowning.

Hastings shrugged. "Anything is possible, I guess. But we have to deal with the problem we're faced with. A feral shifter with a jones for Sullivan Lane." Hastings sat back and sighed. "Well, at least he has good taste. Sullivan Lane is a babe."

Nick growled. He couldn't help it. The sound just came out. A challenge, and an expression of acute displeasure. Hastings looked at him sharply.

"Sorry, Captain. She's *my* babe," Nick admitted, his inner cat wanting to yowl in triumph as his human side admitted it out loud for the first time. "She just doesn't know it yet."

"Yikes," Hastings said, his eyebrows rising in surprise. "I don't know whether to congratulate you or offer condolences. I will, however, wish you luck." Hastings extended his hand across the table, and Nick took it for a strong shake, and a sign of Hastings' good wishes.

"Thanks, Captain," Nick replied, grinning.

"Call me Collin," Hastings said offhandedly. "We're out of the army now."

"Then, I'm Nick," he told the werehawk in just as friendly a tone.

It looked like they were going to be able to work well together, and Nick was relieved. Sometimes, officers were asses, and Nick hadn't really been around Hastings enough to know whether he was a jerk or not. So far, it looked like he definitely *wasn't* a jerk, which boded well for their mission.

They spent the next thirty minutes discussing the particulars of the security coverage. Nick went into detail about Sal's schedule, and what they had planned to keep her safe while she made her public appearances. Nick didn't, however, tell Hastings about the fact that Sal might still have damaging evidence of a jaguar shifter transforming on video. No, that was a secret he could not share with just anyone. Not yet.

If he managed to defuse the situation, then okay. If it turned out she didn't have video, or if she had no intention of talking to anyone about what she had seen, then fine. He could chalk up the incident as a non-problem, and they could all get on with their lives. If, however, she managed to somehow make the alleged video public, then he was up shit's creek already anyway, and it didn't matter if he'd told Hastings or not.

For now, Nick was just going to keep that particular problem to himself. He'd either find the video and erase it or have a heart-to-heart with Sal about her intentions. Of course, if she was as attracted to him as he was to her, and she agreed to be his mate, then it wouldn't matter if she had video evidence or not.

Human mates were allowed to know the secret. Their love for their mate and children would keep their silence on the subject, as it had for millennia. The mate bond was stronger than anything humans had, or felt, for each other. It was sacred. Special. Soul-deep.

If Sal was his mate, she wouldn't expose his people. She couldn't do that and truly be his mate. It was…unthinkable.

CHAPTER 5

When Sal woke, she didn't know where she was. The room was beautiful in an Asian-opulence sort of way, but it was definitely one she had never seen before.

Nick's place. That's where she was. She remembered now. The horror of the night before made her sit up in bed.

She was still wearing the same loose clothing she had put on the night before. It slithered against the red silk of the sheets. She really looked around at the room and took in the design.

It was a little ostentatious for her tastes, but the red silk didn't look tawdry in this setting. It fit beautifully with the Asian-inspired chrysanthemum motif. Big pink flowers were on the walls, with red and black accents. The furniture was high quality. Black lacquer cabinets and bed frame with red fabrics, like the silk sheets. The curtains were the same bold chrysanthemum pattern as on the walls, bordered with red and hanging on black lacquer rods with decorative finials. The pink was a shade that somehow worked perfectly with the bright red.

Professional design. It had to be. No way had Nick decorated this place himself. She just couldn't picture the rough-and-tumble bodyguard choosing giant chrysanthemums as the basis for a guest room—and definitely not for his master bedroom. She found herself smiling at the mere thought.

Pushing the soft covers back, she swung her legs over the side of the bed and discovered her shoes, put neatly under the bed, just the heels sticking out, so she could readily see them. Nick must be a neatnik, if he'd done that. Her suspicions were confirmed when she also noted her overnight bag on top of the chest at the foot of the bed. It was unopened, but perfectly centered and sitting up straight on the chest, where she could easily find it.

Nick must have brought her in here. The last thing she remembered was sitting down on the plush couch. It had been super comfortable, and she must have fallen asleep, feeling safe at last. Something about Nick gave her that feeling. The other guards were great, but only with Nick did she feel safe enough to sleep without worry.

Of course, last night, that had almost been her undoing. Someone had gotten past all the men stationed in the grounds around her rented house. The man had somehow gotten into her bedroom.

Fear engulfed her once again—less than it had the night before, but still very potent—as she remembered waking up to find a huge form standing mere feet from her bed, looming over her in the dark. She'd seen something flash. A knife? Claws?

Claws? Crap.

Could this have something to do with those kids she'd seen at the director's party? She still wasn't one hundred percent certain she'd seen a boy transformed into a leopard. Maybe the one drink she'd allowed herself at the party had been spiked with something. People didn't really turn into vicious animals, did they?

Then again, she had seen stranger things in her time. She'd heard stories, myths and legends about shapeshifters. Her mother's people had always had such tales. But she hadn't believed them. Not really. She just thought they were stories shared around a campfire or a hearth. Stories to tell children

47

and give them something to fear besides the harsh realities of life.

Few people realized Sullivan Lane was part Navajo. Her mother had distanced herself from her Indian heritage. She'd turned her back on superstition. Or so she'd told Sal during the sane times. The times when her wild magic wasn't causing her to act out in ways the human world found unacceptable.

Sal had often thought that perhaps a Native American shaman could help her mother, but Sal didn't have any connections in the community, and her mother was adamantly against having anything to do with that side of her heritage. Sal had never really understood why, but any time she brought up the idea, it provoked a violent episode, so she'd stopped talking about it.

She hadn't stopped thinking about it, though. Getting help for her mom was still very important to her, but Sal didn't quite know where to turn. She'd hoped that maybe now that she had real money coming in, she might be able to use some of it to track down real help for her mother, but she didn't quite know where to start.

Sal had asked around a bit about the boy from the valet service, but she hadn't been able to learn anything useful. Not even his name. She wasn't even sure what she would do if she found him. How could a kid help her find help for her mother? Even if she wasn't hallucinating and the kid really was a mythical skinwalker?

That's what they called shapeshifters of Navajo legend. Sal had heard her mother use the term, but always with great fear. Sal had looked it up on the internet and what she'd found had left her feeling a bit of trepidation. Skinwalkers were said to have committed truly evil deeds in order to gain the power of shapeshifting. It wasn't a benevolent thing, so if she really had seen the kid turn into a giant spotted cat, she probably should steer clear. She'd arrived at that conclusion after her web search and was glad she hadn't been able to track down any information on the young man. Better to let sleeping dogs—or cats, in this case—lie.

But what if the man who had come in through her balcony door had been a skinwalker? What if he was there to silence her? Or threaten her?

He'd certainly done that. She'd been scared out of her wits, though she'd had presence of mind enough to locate the loaded gun she had kept under her pillow since the decapitated squirrel had shown up on her doorstep. The man—creature—had reared back when she pointed the gun at him. And then, he'd fled.

Thank God.

She didn't really want to shoot anyone, but she would have had to pull the trigger if he had continued to menace her. To this moment, she wasn't completely sure she would have been able to do that. Target shooting was one thing, and she enjoyed it very much, but actually shooting a person was quite another. She'd never had cause to shoot anyone before, and she hoped she never came that close ever again.

There were two doors in the room. She tried one, finding an attached bathroom decorated in much the same style as the bedroom. She used the facilities but delayed taking a shower—though she badly wanted one—until she knew more about where she was and if the situation had changed since she fell asleep.

Using the hairbrush she'd packed last night, she made herself mostly presentable and tried the other door, which led, as expected, to the hallway, which then led to the living room she remembered. The main area was somewhat open-concept, so she easily spotted Nick and an unknown man seated at the marble-topped island that separated the kitchen from the living room. Both men stopped talking and turned to look at her as she emerged from the hallway.

"How are you feeling, Miss Lane?" Nick asked politely.

"Much better, thanks. I just wanted to check in before I shower, in case something's changed since last night." She moved closer, eyeing the strange man.

"Nothing new to report, except the arrival of Collin Hastings," Nick told her, gesturing to the other man, who stood and stretched out a hand, offering her a friendly smile. "Collin is an associate who owns one of the premier private investigation firms in the country. He's agreed to personally oversee the hunt for whoever breached our security last night."

Sal shook the other man's hand, appraising him as she learned his role. He had a crooked nose that looked as if it had been broken more than once, but oddly, that didn't detract from his otherwise handsome face. He was built on the muscular side, like Nick, but he was a little taller and leaner. He looked almost lanky but still presented a strong appearance of competence, strength and determination.

"Thank you for agreeing to help with this," Sal said politely.

"Glad I was free and able to come," he replied. "Please forgive my casual attire. When I heard what had happened, I took the first flight and didn't stop to get clothes. I'm based out of Las Vegas these days, but Nick and I had a meeting planned for this afternoon anyway. After the incident last night, we moved up the time. I'm only sorry I wasn't here sooner."

"Speaking of which…" Nick came around the island and stood before her, his expression solemn. "On behalf of myself and my team, I have to apologize to you, Miss Lane. I've spent the past few hours figuring out exactly what happened, and I can assure you, it will not happen again. We failed you. I failed you." His head lowered in an expression of shame and regret that she hated to see on this powerful man. "If you'll give me a chance, I promise to do better from here on out."

"Oh, Nick…" She wanted to reach out to him, but Collin's presence stifled her impulses. "I don't blame you or any of your men for what happened. How are they, by the way? Is everybody okay?"

"Concussions," Nick reported, his mouth held in a tight line. "Those guys won't be on duty for a while. We're replacing the team with people from Collin's outfit. They have special skills that make them a better choice for now."

Sal looked back at the other man and then met Nick's gaze. "I trust your judgment. I trust *you*, Nick. Don't worry about yesterday. Let's just move forward from here, okay?"

"You're being very gracious about this," Nick told her candidly. "You have every right to fire us all and find somebody else. Most people in your situation would do exactly that."

"I think you've already figured out that I'm not like most people in Hollywood, and frankly, this situation is complicated. I think you've all handled it as well as you could to this point. I don't think any other company could do better." Especially if skinwalkers were involved, Sal thought very carefully to herself. She didn't know of any traditional security company that could deal with something like that.

Nick wanted so much to take her in his arms and just hold her tight. Tell her everything would be all right from here on out. But of course, he couldn't do that. It wouldn't be professional and Collin freaking Hastings was sitting three feet away, watching them like the hawk that shared his soul.

"Well, my boss will be pleased to hear that," Nick said instead, backing away from her. He needed space to think clearly.

"So, what's on the agenda for today?" she asked, surprising him.

"Uh…" Nick tried to think fast. "We'll be going over schedules and assignments." He gestured toward Collin, who had retaken his seat at the kitchen island. "I believe your public relations people had you scheduled for a dress fitting. Something about choosing a gown for an upcoming awards show."

"Oh, yeah." Sal didn't look too cheerful at that idea. "They want me to wear some designer label and borrowed diamonds. I'm going to push that off for a day or two. Is it okay if I just stay here for today? I mean, I don't want to impose on you, but I don't think I can face that house again right now, and I've already been through one move. It's not as easy and fast as they lead you to believe."

"Well, that answers one of my questions. You want to move out of that house." Nick nodded in approval. The rented mansion was too hard to secure against a feral shifter. That had already been proven.

"Yeah. After last night, I just won't feel safe there. Sorry."

"Don't be sorry. I was actually going to try to convince you to leave there. Our perimeter was already breached once. The place isn't secure enough for the situation you're in right now." Nick frowned when he saw her expression turn fearful. He shouldn't have reminded her of her problems. "You're doing the right thing. We'll find you a place that's easier to secure while Collin and his team track down our perp and make certain he doesn't bother you again."

"You can do that? I mean, I thought the police..."

"We assist the police from time to time," Hastings put in. "In this sort of case, they couldn't provide the kind of coverage you'd need, and they probably don't have the manpower to follow every lead, the way we do. But don't worry, we'll interface with the officials, and we won't do anything to put you in jeopardy legally. Everything we do will be above board and according to the law."

Nick personally thought Hastings was taking a few liberties with the truth as Sal would understand it, but he didn't say anything. It was pretty clever, though. Hastings would do everything according to the law that governed *shifters*. The laws handed down by the Lords and the Mother of All. He wasn't technically lying, though Sal probably understood his words to reference the laws of man, which had little effect on those shifters that lived in secret among humans.

"Feel free to stay right here as long as you like," Nick put in helpfully.

Frankly, he wouldn't mind if she stayed with him for the rest of their lives, but he was getting ahead of himself. He had to remember to take things slow. She was human, after all.

"All right, then." She turned to head back toward the guest room. "I'm going to take a shower. I'll be out in twenty minutes if you need me for anything."

"Take your time. We have lots of planning to do," Hastings told her.

Nick was momentarily struck speechless at the idea that she was going to take a shower. Naked. Wet and soapy. Slick. Warm. Luscious.

Damn.

"Earth to Nick. Come in, Nick. Over."

Nick looked over to find Hastings chuckling at his own little joke.

"Kindly stow it. Sir."

Nick went to the refrigerator and was sorely tempted to pull out an ice cold beer, but it was too early in the morning. Even for him. He opted for a bottle of cold water, instead. Maybe the icy bite of the water hitting his system would help cool him down.

For the next half hour, Nick discussed all the facets of the operation with Hastings that couldn't be talked about in front of his guest. He kept one ear on the hallway, alert to any sound that might indicate she was coming back into the living room.

Nick did his very best not to think about all that hot water, and the suds… Oh, man. The suds. Slicking down over her wet skin.

Yeah. He cleared his throat. He really had to focus on the task at hand. Right now, that was the perpetually smirking hawk shifter in front of him. Fucking Hastings, man. He could read between the lines. The man wasn't stupid, after all. He'd be of no use to Nick or Sal if he were.

But it made his inner cat's back arch in discomfort to know this relative stranger could read him so easily. The beginning of a courtship was a delicate time for any shifter, when the protective instincts of his animal nature were riled up, even more so than usual. It was all about protecting the mate.

From danger. From feral shifters, in this particular case. And even from Hastings and all the other men assigned to watch her. That they watched—and perhaps had covetous thoughts about her—was driving kitty mad.

It didn't help that half the male population of the United States, if not the world, had seen her in the movies. A good portion of them had probably lusted after her. Fantasized about her.

Not good. Not good at all. The cat wanted to scratch all their eyes out and piss on their innards for lusting after his mate.

Nick would have to get a grip on his jealousy if he was going to have any chance of a relationship with Sal. She was a movie star. There was no way to put that genie back into the bottle. He'd have to suck it up, or move on. And giving up wasn't in his vocabulary.

Time for the sucking to begin.

And just on that rather loaded thought, he heard her door click open followed by the soft patter of her feet on the carpet. Hastings heard it, too, and their discussion immediately shifted to more general topics.

Hastings left a short while later, already on the case. Nick knew he was going to arrange for more coverage of the building from his people—both in the air, and on the ground. The task was made simpler by the fact that Sal had decided to stay put for the day.

Nick offered to make her breakfast, but she declined, opting instead for a cup of tea and an orange. He hoped she wasn't one of those women who never ate. He liked her figure and all, but she was too skinny. He worried about hurting her when they got around to intimacy. He'd have to be super careful with her.

Of course, she probably kept herself so thin because of the movie career. He'd heard it said that the camera added pounds, and most of the starlet wannabes were rail thin in person, though they looked normal on film.

Sal wasn't that bad. Not like some of the walking skeletons

he'd seen since arriving in Los Angeles. Sal had curves. Luscious ones. But she was also thin by shifter standards. Maybe it was because she was human. Nick hadn't really been involved with that many human women in his time. Mostly, he cavorted with shifter women, who had more meat on their bones and could take a hard loving. He'd have to tread carefully until he knew what Sal could handle and what she liked.

But he didn't mind. He'd do anything for her.

She just didn't know it yet.

CHAPTER 6

Around ten o'clock in the morning, Hastings—attired in new clothing he'd sourced from somewhere—escorted an assistant from Sal's agent's office up to the apartment. Nick met them at the door and double checked the assistant's identification. Sal verified that she knew this person, and he allowed them a few moments in the living room—although he kept an eye on them from the kitchen area—to discuss the changes in her schedule.

Nick noted that the woman called Sal by the nickname he'd seen in some of the tabloids—Sully. Somehow, it didn't seem to fit and he wondered about the different nicknames she seemed to use. Was he the only one who'd been invited to call her Sal? And if so, why?

Nick shook off the question for another time. It wasn't really that important, after all, what Sullivan Lane wanted to be called. The most important thing right now was her safety.

The assistant had also dropped off a small box filled with paper. Scripts, she'd said when she'd handed the box off to Sal. Nick sniffed the air cautiously, though he hid his actions from the humans. He scented only paper. Nothing dangerous.

After the assistant left, Sal sat on the couch in a late morning shaft of sunlight and started to read the contents of the box. Nick sat at the kitchen island, working on his own plans and staff schedules, though Hastings was handling the actual scheduling for his people. Still, it was up to Nick to make it all work. There were still the men from the day and evening shifts from Halibut to work into the mix. Not all of them, but a few would be helpful on the ground, freeing up Hastings' people for the aerial work they excelled at.

Not all of Hastings' people were bird shifters, though he'd brought mostly hawks with him on this particular mission. Still, it was said Hastings hired all kinds of shifters, as long as they had superior investigative skills, fighting ability, experience in field work, and would have the qualifications he required. He took only the best of the best and took on some of the most difficult cases in the paranormal community.

For today, and especially tonight, he and his team were covering the security on the condo. The Halibut guys had the day off, but they'd be worked back into the schedule tomorrow afternoon, when Sal returned to her busy routine of appearances, meetings, fittings and gala events. The Halibut men were the experts in those kinds of situations, and Hastings' people liked to keep a lower profile than being the center of a paparazzi scrum all trying to get at Sal.

Nick made a call to Linelli late in the morning to report on progress. Linelli offered to come over and talk to the client, but Nick told him not to. Everything was under control. He hoped.

When he returned to the main area of the condo, Sal was still there, reading. She'd gone through about half the box of scripts, separating them into piles. She was reading again, so he went past without interrupting her. He'd make lunch. Maybe she'd eat some, if he could figure out what might tempt her.

That thought in mind, he went to the fridge and pulled out ingredients. He had a few dishes he'd liked enough to learn how to cook. Chicken was one of those things he could prepare with some confidence, in several different ways. He opted for a simple sauce of pineapple, soy sauce, and a few spices that wouldn't add a lot of extra calories. Maybe she'd like that, and he would feel good about feeding her something healthy and filling.

He tossed a salad for good measure and put some rice in the cooker. She might not go for the carbs, but he'd present the option and see what he could learn about her eating habits. He'd have to get to know what she liked if they were going to spend the rest of their lives together.

When it was ready, he didn't even have to call her. Apparently, the scents wafting from the kitchen area had captured her attention all by themselves.

"Something smells yummy," she said, sniffing the air as she came into the kitchen, carrying her tea mug. "I didn't realize you could cook."

"I'm full of surprises," Nick answered, plating the chicken and rice and setting it on the table.

"Indeed you are," she agreed, following the food as if drawn to it. "And I'm very glad of it, because right now, I'm famished." She had a big smile on her face that made his heart feel light. "Is there anything I can do to help?"

"No. Just sit down. I've got this," he said gently, glad he'd made the effort. Feeding one's mate was a primal need for a shifter. His inner cat hadn't been happy when she had declined breakfast.

Now, the jaguar was sitting at attention, watching her every move. It wanted to see for itself that she was taking care of herself. Eating properly. Appreciating good food.

Nick shouldn't have worried. When he placed the serving dishes on the table, Sal went for the rice first, taking a huge scoop over which she placed a few cuts of the chicken. She'd taken a healthy portion for a small female, which pleased him to no end. He had to laugh as she bypassed the salad, though she did put a small portion on the side of her plate, taking half the cherry tomatoes he'd used as a garnish. And she didn't pick the oil and vinegar set he'd put out, but instead grabbed the ranch dressing bottle he'd put closer to his own plate. She didn't use a lot, but she definitely put a dollop of it on her tomatoes that had a little bit of lettuce underneath.

"Why are you smiling?" She looked up from her plate, giving him a sideways look.

"I guess I'm just surprised to see a woman in this town actually eating carbs. I half-thought you might grab the entire salad and say that was all you needed."

She laughed, the sound unexpectedly touching him deep inside. "Oh, I like my food. Probably too much, if you go by the standards in this crazy town. But when I'm not actively filming, I don't starve myself. If I have to cut back for a role, I do it, but I don't like it. Mama likes to *eat.*"

They both chuckled at her exaggerated tone, and then, there was only the sounds of cutlery and chewing for a few minutes. She wasn't kidding, he was glad to see. She went for the chicken and rice first, only occasionally adding in a creamy tomato or a spring of lettuce.

"This is fantastic," she enthused at one point, when she came up for air. "I didn't realize how hungry I was. This morning, I just couldn't face a big breakfast, though it was sweet of you to offer. I just felt sick to my stomach when I remembered last night."

"Understandable," Nick said quietly. He'd been insensitive, he realized.

She was human. Unused to violent situations that were his stock in trade. She'd probably never been threatened like that before. He should have thought about that and been more understanding.

"I'm glad to see you're feeling better now," he added while she reapplied herself to her lunch.

"Yeah, getting back to work helped," she told him a minute later, after she had chewed and swallowed. "Some of those scripts are really good. My agent wants me to lock in at least three more deals while I'm *hot*, as he put it. He claims he can get me top dollar, right now, while the timing is right. I'm not keen on the idea of tying myself up for that long, but I told him I would at least read through the scripts he'd selected. I'm glad I agreed now because some of those are juicy roles and incredible stories that will probably make great movies."

"Three movie projects?" Nick asked. "What kind of time commitment is that? A year? Two years?"

"Oh, my part in filming only takes a month or two, depending on how involved the character is in the story. Depending on when they want to start filming—they have to secure funding, locations, costume design, sets, travel, and all that kind of thing—three movies could be done in six months or a year. But they'd probably do a staggered release because you don't want to over-saturate the market. Too many Sullivan Lane movies coming out all at once might compete against each other."

"I suppose a lot of planning goes into each project," Nick surmised.

"Yeah, scheduling is one of the biggest considerations. Timing is everything in this business, or so I've been told." She cleaned her plate and seemed to be eyeing the rest of the chicken.

Nick had to stifle a laugh. He'd been worried about nothing. She ate. She wasn't a foolish woman. His mate was strong of will, body and mind. She was perfect.

"You can have the rest, if you want. I had a big working breakfast with Collin," he told her.

Her eyes lit up. "I hope you don't think I'm a pig, but this was so good…" She went ahead and dumped the remainder of the rice and chicken on to her plate.

Nick decided to gather the empty dishes while she finished her seconds. He didn't want to make her uncomfortable, sitting there staring at her while she ate.

After lunch, she went back to her reading while he cleaned up. He'd declined her offer of help with the dishes because he didn't think he could take sharing the limited space in the kitchen without kissing her some more. He wanted to kiss her again more than anything, but it was too soon. He had to be patient or he'd scare her away, and that was the last thing he wanted to do.

In the middle of the afternoon, Linelli himself showed up at Nick's door. It wasn't unexpected. Linelli was the point man from Halibut—one of the three partners who had signed the contract with Miss Lane. He had a vested interest in keeping her happy and making sure she was all right. Frankly, Nick had expected Linelli to show up sooner. The fact that he'd waited this long meant that he trusted Nick more than Nick had realized. Oddly touched by the trust Linelli had placed in him, Nick ushered him into the opulent apartment.

Linelli whistled low, between his teeth as he got a look around. "Man. I must be paying you too much."

"It's a rental," Nick told his human friend. "And Mark's paying for it."

"You're still working for Mark Pepard?" Linelli asked, though he probably already knew the answer.

"He's my best friend," Nick answered honestly. "Even if I'm not officially on the payroll, I'd walk through fire for that guy."

While true, that wasn't even the half of it. Mark Pepard was the jaguar Alpha. Nick was loyal to him for that reason, but also because they'd grown up together and really were best friends. They were as close as brothers, though Nick was glad to give Mark and his new mate some space, right now, while they celebrated their honeymoon and Nick took care of this little problem for the Clan.

"So, what you're saying is that not all billionaires as assholes," Linelli summed up with a smirk.

"In my experience, definitely not. At least not Mark. And his wife is good people, too," Nick put in.

"Yeah, I'd heard he'd gotten hitched. She's from old money, right? A society gal?" Linelli was clearly fishing, but Nick was happy enough to spread the news that Mark's mate was a straight arrow.

"She's a professional, actually. Her father was rich, but he'd had a reversal of fortune in recent years, so she became an architect. She designs houses for a living—mostly for that elite social circle her family was part of, true enough—but she's not a snob. Far from it. She's actually very sweet." Nick didn't want to think about the hard time he'd given the woman when he'd thought she might be involved in a plot to assassinate Mark.

They'd both agreed to forget their first meeting, but he still thought about it and winced every once in a while. He'd been rough on her. Even threatened to make her *disappear*. He really hoped she could truly forgive him in time, but for now, he still sensed a certain reticence when she had to deal with him.

The two men entered the living room to find Sal still sitting on the couch, reading. She looked up and smiled when she saw Nick, lighting his whole world.

"Miss Lane, please let me express my regret over the incident last night." Linelli launched into his appease-the-client shtick, and Nick just stood back and watched. This was Linelli's show for the moment. It was Linelli's business reputation on the line. Nick wouldn't interfere.

He watched them chat back and forth for a bit. Linelli being apologetic and Sal being forgiving and very gracious. He realized she really wasn't upset with Linelli or the guys from Halibut, which was very big of her, but Nick wondered why she was so ready to forgive the oversight that had let her be menaced by a madman in her own bedroom.

Was there something else going on here than what appeared on the surface? Nick frowned. Something wasn't kosher, but he was very hesitant to accuse Sal of anything. She was his mate, after all. That fact alone earned his loyalty. He was convinced—based solely on instinct—that whatever she was hiding, it wasn't something evil. His mate could never be evil.

Nick let Linelli sit with her while he went into the room he was using as a study and got his laptop. While Nick might prefer pen and paper, Linelli was a computer guy all the way. Nick would show Linelli the details of the plan he and Hastings had come up with and email the big-picture items. Nick didn't trust the details to the uncertain security of the

World Wide Web. Not when dealing with systems he hadn't had vetted by his own Clan's tech experts.

Halibut may think they had state-of-the-art protection on their electronic systems, but Nick wasn't taking any chances. Luckily, Linelli was content to let Nick run this show the way he saw fit, and the minutiae of scheduling each and every operative wasn't something Linelli needed to know beforehand. He understood operational security as well as Nick did, and was willing to give Nick the authority to make those decisions on his own.

When Nick came back out to the living room, Sal was gone. He could hear her faint footsteps going down the hall toward her bedroom and didn't worry. She was giving them some privacy to discuss business matters. His mate was considerate that way. And as long as she was in the apartment with Hastings' people in the sky and on the ground, she was as safe as Nick could make her.

Linelli left after the meeting, and Hastings reported that his first shift of operatives hadn't seen anything or caught any scents. He'd already dispatched a ground-based team of shifters—a werewolf and a werebear—to see if they could follow the scent trail left by last night's interloper at the mansion, but the trail had gone cold after a mile or two when the feral had taken time to cross a few highways then go down into a culvert. The residue of water in the culvert had dissipated the scent enough that the tracker team couldn't reacquire the trail, no matter how many times they tried.

Nick wasn't happy with the results and would have preferred to give his own nose a try at the scent trail, but he couldn't leave Sal. He had to trust that Hastings' people had done their best and move on from there. He'd get another crack at the feral. And with any luck, next time, he'd get to the bastard before he got near Sal again.

She came out of her room after Hastings had left, and Nick was just finishing up with the laptop, sending the overview report on last night's incident to Linelli's email address. He looked up, and the sight of her stole his breath. Damn. She was not only gorgeous, but as he'd gotten to know her over these past hours, he found himself attracted to everything about her. Her quick wit, her no-nonsense attitude, even her willingness to lay low today while they sorted out her security arrangements.

A stereotypical spoiled Hollywood starlet wouldn't have done that. Nick had been around a few bratty humans in his time, and he knew that type would insist on having things their own way, regardless of the difficulties that might create for others. Not Sal. She seemed to put other people's comfort before her own. She was a kind soul that hadn't been damaged by the Hollywood environment. At least, not yet.

If he had his way, she never would be. She was his to protect, not just now, but for the rest of their lives—if he could get her to agree to those terms. He had time yet, to figure out the best approach. They'd only met a few days ago, but already, she trusted him with her safety, and given the choice, she had opted to stay with him, in the condo. That meant a lot to him.

"What do you feel like having for dinner?" he asked. "I thought I'd order in, since I got sidetracked with work and lost track of time."

"Oh, I don't expect you to cook for me," she told him quickly. "I could cook..." she said, then trailed off, glancing at the clock.

"That's okay. I know a few different restaurants that deliver. I know a great burger place, Chinese, Mexican, a good steak house..." He ticked off all the choices.

"Burgers sound good," she told him, surprising him yet again. Most women he'd known would opt for something more exotic, but his own first choice would have been the burgers, so they were definitely on the same page.

"Burgers, it is," he replied with a smile. He reached into a drawer and pulled out a stack of printed menus. Locating the one for the burger joint, he handed it to her before putting the others back in the drawer.

All of the menus were from local establishments owned and operated by shapeshifters of one kind or another. Nick had vetted them all personally, patronizing their restaurants one at a time since he'd moved in. He trusted them to deliver wholesome, delicious food in a timely manner.

Sal made her choices, checking off items on the menu with a pencil that had been lying on the table. Nick was pleased to see that she didn't skimp and even ordered dessert. He called in the order and was given a delivery time of forty-five minutes. He then called down to the men on duty, to give them the heads up that they would be receiving a delivery.

"I've got one more script to get through," Sal told Nick as she stood from her seat at the table. "I'll probably be able to finish it before the dinner arrives. Just give me a shout when it gets here, okay?"

Nick agreed, watching her walk away. She really had the nicest ass. He couldn't wait to get his hands on her, but he understood the need to win over her heart, as well. He knew he could seduce her body. He'd never left a woman wanting in his life. But he wanted it all. Her luscious body, her quick mind, her tender heart, and her very soul.

CHAPTER 7

Dinner was delicious. The burgers were perfectly cooked and seasoned, and the fries were crisp and tasty. The dessert Sal had chosen—a slice of New York-style cheesecake—melted in her mouth and probably went straight to her hips, but she didn't care.

The pressure to stay rail thin now that she'd had some success in the movies was getting on her nerves. She had never aspired to be a model. She'd never been a fitness freak, though she enjoyed a healthy lifestyle. But she was never going to be a size zero. It just wasn't something she would or could do. So be it.

The movie-going public and also people who seemed to think her newfound success gave them the right to tell her how to live, what to eat, how she should look, and all the other stuff were just going to have to chill. Sal decided those things for herself. Thank you very much.

Maybe she was going through a bit of a rebellious phase. The fame was something completely new, and not altogether welcome. Especially when it brought baggage along with it like crazy expectations and potentially violent stalkers. Yeah, maybe fame wasn't all it was cracked up to be.

Although, at least one good thing had come out of her recent problems. Nick. Nick was the good thing in her life right now. The one thing she could cling to in the midst of her turmoil. Without him, she would probably be a basket case right about now.

He was just such a commanding presence. Such a strong man—both physically and in a spiritual way she couldn't quite define. There was just something about him. Something that made her trust him in ways she hadn't trusted anyone before.

He was easy on the eyes, as well. A regular hunk. She couldn't imagine why he didn't have a live-in girlfriend. Were all the women in this town blind as well as stupid? Nick was a hottie, and he was smart, too. Decisive and manly in ways that made her tingle in unmentionable places.

She was grateful to him for giving her a place to hide. He hadn't needed to open up his home to her. She knew she was imposing on his better nature, but she really didn't want to be separated from him right now. He was her port in the storm. Her rock. Her anchor. He was helping her stay calm, just by his mere presence.

She felt a little bad about invading his space this way, but he truly didn't seem to mind. She'd heard him talking to Mr. Linelli about the condo being a rental, and she'd recognized the name they had bandied about. Mark Pepard was one of the richest men in the country and had a mysterious reputation.

No wonder Nick had seemed so familiar to her. She'd seen the pictures on the pages of the tabloids, just like everyone else. Mark Pepard, flying off all over the world on adventures and humanitarian missions, always surrounded by people from his companies. And always nearby, right next to him in many of the photos, was Nick. An unnamed companion, or bodyguard, or security agent.

After hearing Nick's conversation, she now understood that he wasn't just another employee to Mark Pepard. They were friends. That put Nick in a whole other social stratum. If he hobnobbed with billionaires, what was he doing playing at being a private security guard for a newcomer to the Hollywood scene?

Her instincts were clamoring. Something wasn't quite right with the situation, but it also didn't feel threatening. Nick felt absolutely safe to her. As if he would protect her with his life, if necessary. And he felt good to the core. Not an ounce of evil could last around this man. She trusted those instincts of hers when it came to things like good and evil.

But the puzzle remained. Why was he here? Why had he taken the time—and the job—to protect her? Strange as it seemed, she began to wonder if he was a fan. Maybe he'd liked her performance on the screen and wanted to get closer to her.

While flattering, that was also a bit of a creepy thought. She didn't think the scenario fit. It had to be something else, but she couldn't imagine what.

Having finished dinner, they retired to the living room area. There was a big screen television hiding behind a painting that slid down out of sight when Nick pressed a button on the complicated-looking remote control. Everything about this condo was top notch and high tech. Expensive.

Which made sense if the place was truly intended for someone of Mark Pepard's stature. The fact that Nick seemed right at home here spoke of a vast experience with wealth that she, herself, had never had until recently.

"Shall we watch the news? See what's going on in the world?" Nick asked quietly.

She agreed, and he put on the news station that she preferred. Impressive. Had he somehow intuited her preferences, or did they have the same taste and political leanings? Either way, she gave him a point on her mental tally sheet in his favor.

On the commercial breaks, they talked about current events and exchanged points of view on the various topics of interest from around the world. Nick's firsthand knowledge of the political situations in some very remote foreign countries gave her pause. Nick was a world traveler. A true citizen of the globe.

She was just a gal who had gotten lucky with a good movie role. She had never traveled outside the United States, though she had gotten a few offers in recent weeks to film in Europe and other exotic locations.

She had been a little giddy at the idea, but then, reality had set in. She couldn't stray too far from where her mother was being held. Even if her mother would never be free again, she was still her mother. Her flesh and blood. Sal would visit every chance she could and be available should her mother need her. It was the right thing to do.

Still, she enjoyed talking with Nick. And when the news was over and they put on a documentary about UFOs and aliens visiting the earth in the distant past, she discovered they shared another interest, and what were probably wild imaginations.

They sat together on the couch, and Sal couldn't help but want to get closer to him. He was so warm. So solid. So amazingly handsome and attractive in every way. And the more she got to know him, the more attractive he became.

A lot of men had given her the opposite experience. Familiarity often bred contempt. It was refreshing and reassuring to discover that getting to know a guy didn't always mean disliking him and his ideas.

Quite the opposite. At least with Nick. She'd already suspected he was a special case. She was glad to have her instincts proven correct.

At one point, he got up and made tea for them both. When he came back, he sat much closer on the couch, and she grew warm—and not just from the tea.

When he finished with his tea, he put the mug down on the coffee table then leaned back, placing his arm along the top of the sofa—behind her. Just a little closer, and he'd have that muscular arm around her shoulders. And from there…

Damn. If yearning could make it happen, she'd already be in bed with him by now. But he was clearly being a gentleman and exercising caution. While she appreciated that, she was also growing a bit impatient.

Never one to make the first move on a guy, Sal found herself wanting to do so with Nick. Heck, she more than wanted to. She was going to do it. If he didn't make a move in the next five minutes, she was going to—

Her thoughts were cut off by the feel of his arm around her shoulders, turning her to face him. She cooperated fully, moving to meet him halfway. The look in his eyes made her breath catch. There was a swirl of energy there that she thought she saw. But maybe she was wrong. She couldn't be sure.

"Tell me to go to hell if you want," he whispered, his head dipping closer to hers. "But I've been dying to kiss you again."

"Then, what are you waiting for?" she whispered back, being about as daring as she'd ever been with a man. Nick's smile was answer enough, and it made her insides melt into a little puddle of need. Then, he moved even closer and his lips met hers.

Magic. That's what it felt like. Pure, good, clean, powerful magic.

But it couldn't be. She'd never experienced the good side of magic, but she had heard it existed. Somewhere.

Nick was a bodyguard, not a mage. He was just a man. Not a monster.

And he kissed like a dream.

Kissing Sal was everything Nick had thought it would be...and more. She fit in his arms like she was born to be there. She tasted of sweet nectar and goodness, and she felt soft, feminine and perfect against him. Her passion matched his, and he forgot all the nonsense he'd been telling himself about how she was human and wasn't as sturdy as shifter women. It was all bunk.

When she grabbed his shirt and demanded more, who was he to argue?

He let her have her way. Her nimble fingers tore at his clothes, seeking skin. And then, her hands were on his chest, smoothing over his pecs and down to his abdomen. His breath hitched as she hit a sensitive spot. All the while, her tongue dueled with his.

She was molten fire in his arms, demanding and passionate in a way he hadn't expected but was thrilled to discover. She would be a wildcat in bed, if this was any indication. Still, he didn't push too hard or too fast. He let her have all the control for now. He would revel in learning her preferences and satisfying her every need. He knew his patience now would reap rewards for the rest of their lives together.

Sal had just pushed him down onto his back on the couch when Nick heard the sound of rustling feathers coming from the balcony. His sensitive ears picked up the soft sounds, even beyond the closed glass doors.

Fucking Hastings. It had to be him. Nobody else would dare interrupt what could so clearly be seen through the glass doors.

Hmm. Maybe Hastings was trying to remind him that Sal wouldn't be pleased to discover she'd been putting on a show for the hawk shifters on duty just beyond the glass. Because, she would find out...eventually.

Damn. She was human. She wouldn't understand that having sex in view of others wasn't that big a deal among shifters. She'd probably be embarrassed, and she might take it out on Nick. Scratch that. She would definitely take it out on him.

She'd make him pay because he was the informed one here. He should know better. And more than that—he'd vowed to protect her.

Fuck.

Nick pulled away, trying to figure out what he could say to make her understand. She was clingy, which, in other circumstances, would make him growl with appreciation. Right now, however, it only caused more difficulties for him.

He tried to untangle her arms from his body as gently as he could. When she finally got the message that he was calling a halt, she let go like he was on fire. Damn.

He could read hurt in her shuttered gaze, scent emotional pain and embarrassment. He cursed under his breath.

"Honey, I'm on duty here. This isn't right. I can't take advantage of the situation like this. Please understand." He tried to put all the tenderness he was feeling into his voice, but she still smelled sad and angry. At him? At herself? Either way, he didn't like it.

He pulled her resisting body into a loose embrace and tried to soothe her. "Please don't be angry. And don't take this as some kind of rejection. It's not. It's *so* not." He chuckled, rubbing her arm gently. "I just can't do this right now. It's not that I don't want to. I most emphatically do. The timing here is just off." He pulled back to look into her eyes. The tension in her shoulders had eased somewhat, and she seemed to have calmed down a little.

Her cheeks were flushed with a mix of residual passion and probably a bit of embarrassment, but at least she was meeting his gaze. Her expression was still somewhat tight and shuttered, but her eyes met his with a hint of defiance. Good. And bad. He'd have some work to do later, to make this up to her, but for now, she was taking the unintentional rejection as well as possible.

"Like I said, I'm on duty. In fact, I've got to report to Linelli in about…" He made a show of checking his watch. "Damn. I should've called him five minutes ago." As if on cue, his phone rang. "And I bet that's him wondering why I'm slacking off."

Finally, a spark of humor edged out the hurt in her gaze. "You'd better answer that before he sends in the Marines."

A joke. Praise be, the Mother of All. His girl recovered quickly. That was a good trait in a mate. Especially *his* mate, because Nick didn't have the most stable of professions and often had to stop on a dime and change direction.

"I'm sorry, honey. You don't know *how* sorry." He stood from the couch and headed to the marble-topped island that separated the kitchen area from the living room. He'd left his laptop and phone there. He picked up the phone and hit the go button, identifying himself in a terse tone. "Balam."

"I stashed my stuff behind the big planter at the far end of your patio. Sorry for the interruption, but I heard your explanation and figured a timely phone call would help." Hastings' voice was both amused and smug over the line.

The bastard had shifted to human out of sight from the balcony doors. "Thanks, boss," Nick placed a slight emphasis on the last word that wouldn't be lost on the hawk shifter.

Sure enough, Hastings chuckled. "I like the sound of that. The great and powerful Nick Balam working for me instead of the other way around."

"Don't get used to it," Nick practically growled as he watched Sal beat a strategic retreat from the living room, back toward her bedroom. "But thanks all the same for the reminder. She would have been even angrier with me when she found out you and your people were watching us."

"Yeah, that's what I figured. A few of my guys have mated with humans, and they just have different ideas about what's acceptable behavior and what isn't," Hastings commiserated.

"How's it going out there?" Nick asked, hoping for a change of topic.

"Well, I have some news. Which is why I came in for a landing in the first place. Your perp—or at least, someone who fits all the parameters for your perp—has been spotted in the area. A young colleague of mine noticed someone on the ground who looked like he was following a scent trail. Sniffing very obviously, pausing in odd fits and starts. She came to get me to confirm, but when we returned to the spot where she'd left him, he was gone."

"Where?" Nick asked sharply.

"About a mile away from here, as the hawk flies," Hastings replied just as rapidly.

"Not good." Nick growled. He couldn't help it. His inner cat didn't like the fact that the feral wolf might have found their trail so fast.

"I figured you'd want to know right away. This just happened about ten minutes ago."

"So, he could be closer by now," Nick thought aloud.

"Yeah, but you're in the penthouse, and wolves can't climb for shit," Hastings added. "We've got all the entrances and exits covered—including the unconventional ones like this balcony. I think you'll be okay for tonight, but we should probably make plans to capitalize on this. If we can lure him out of hiding—and he seems damned good at hiding, by the way, because I couldn't find anything to indicate where he'd disappeared to—then maybe we can trap him before anything else happens."

Nick liked the sound of that. They could be proactive rather than reactive, and hopefully keep Sal out of the line of fire completely.

"Do you need me to coordinate?" Nick asked the hawk shifter.

"Frankly, Master Sergeant, since everybody on duty right now is from my crew, you'd only get in the way." Hastings was an honest son of a bitch, Nick would give him that. Nick appreciated the candor, and his already good opinion of Hastings rose another notch.

"Understood, Captain." Nick knew full well his function on this op. He was here as the last line of defense, to keep Sal safe.

If, somehow, the perp got past all those shifters Hastings had set in strategic places—and his air cover—then Nick would have his hands full. Primarily, he was there to herd the client into doing what they wanted her to do. He was also the final barrier between the feral shifter and Sal.

"You keep your eyes on your lady, and your hands to yourself for now," Hastings went on, giving unsolicited advice which Nick could have done without. "Or you'll have us all singing out here."

"Singing?" Nick couldn't resist a hint like that. What were those featherheads up to now?

"Well, she is a movie star, and you are *the bodyguard*. My young friend was doing a really good Whitney Houston impersonation a few hours ago when she heard about this whole setup." Then, Hastings launched into song, with a somewhat credible baritone version of that famous song. "I-eee-Iii will all-lll-lll-wa-ys loooove yooooouuuu—"

Nick hung up on him.

It didn't help that he could hear Hastings laughing on the balcony through the barrier of the glass door. Silly bird.

CHAPTER 8

Sal felt a bit foolish when she was finally alone in the bedroom. She'd all but jumped Nick, and the poor guy was working. On duty. She had probably even gotten him in trouble with his boss.

"Stupid, Sal. Really stupid," she told herself, cringing when she thought about the look on his face as he tried to pry her away from him.

She'd been clinging to him like ivy. Needy in a way she never been before. What was it about Nick Balam that attracted her so strongly? He was handsome, to be sure, but she'd been exposed to some incredibly handsome men in recent years as an actress. She'd even done love scenes with some of them and felt nothing at all beyond a mild disgust with one guy, in particular, who was a slobbery kisser.

Nick, though, he pushed all her *on* buttons. He was considerate, kind, built like a Mack truck, and probably deadly, as well. That should probably had scared her off, but the opposite was true. He drew her in like a magnet, strong, sure and lethal to her peace of mind.

And now, she'd made an utter fool of herself. How was she going to face him again?

She decided to take a long shower. She did her best thinking in the shower, and perhaps she could wash away some of her embarrassment and humiliation. Cleansing water was always good for the soul.

A half hour later, she felt refreshed. Still a bit embarrassed, but the water had helped wash away the mortification and soothed her emotions. It was late enough that she could justify putting on her pajamas and curling up in bed with the remainder of her homework. One last script to read, and then, she could hand the whole box back to her agent with her choices.

The rest would be in her agent's hands to see if deals could be struck for the right timing, the right pay and all the other stuff that went along with it. Sal didn't concern herself with that part of the business. All that mattered was working and making steady money. Supporting herself and her mother's needs had been her only goal for a long, long time.

Now, of course, she had other considerations. Paying for security and making enough to maintain the expected lifestyle. Sure, she wasn't going to live the most ostentatious high life. That really wasn't her style. But it had been impressed upon her that there were now appearances to maintain.

Sal thought it was all very silly, but her agent had been adamant. He'd gotten her this far. She assumed he knew what he was talking about. Still, she wasn't going to waste money on truly frivolous things. Sal was cautious by nature and would remain so, even if she had just hit the lottery career-wise.

She hadn't said goodnight to Nick, which was rude, but she just couldn't face him at the moment. Not after the way they'd parted. Maybe, by morning, her courage would return, but for right now, she was taking the coward's way out and hiding in her room.

Besides, they both had work to do. She thumped the pillow on which she had rested the heavy script and made it stand up better so she could read more comfortably. She just had to get through this one and she could forget all her troubles in sleep.

The next thing Sal knew, she was rousing from a disturbed sleep. The bedside light was still on, but the clock read 3:57 a.m. Something had woken her. The script fell to the floor as she sat up in bed, and she realized she must have fallen asleep while reading it.

She was reaching over the side of the bed for it when all hell broke loose. A crash from above knocked the square air vent downward, into the room, with a resounding bang, and a man... No, a *creature* jumped down from overhead. He must've been in the ventilation shaft. Could things that big really fit in an air duct?

She had no sooner had this incongruous thought when the bedroom door burst open to reveal Nick in all his fighting fury. He was in a ready stance. She recognized the posture from one of the movies she had done early in her career that was heavy on martial arts fighting scenes. She hadn't had to fight, but she'd picked up a few things watching the other actors and specialist instructors who had been brought on set to add realism.

The creature was hairy and had to be over seven feet tall. Nick was well over six feet himself, but this dog-looking thing was even bigger, with nasty teeth and a tapered shape to his jaw that made it look almost like a snout. The closest description she could come up with was that he looked like a creature out of one of those old werewolf horror movies. But werewolves didn't actually exist. Did they?

The werewolf thing had been looking straight at her with swirling yellow glowing eyes. She'd seen the swirl of magic before in her mother's eyes. For a moment, Sal thought maybe her past had caught up with her, but there was no way. Her mother wasn't a werewolf. She'd never changed shape or became hairy. She was a person. Always a person, even when the mad glowing eyes took her over.

This had to be something else, then. But what?

She looked at Nick, but his expression didn't reveal any surprise at all. He just looked pissed. Angry. He seemed to recognize what he faced, which didn't make any sense to her.

How could Nick have seen this kind of thing before?

She knew he was a man of many secrets, but this… This was something…supernatural.

The two males were caught in that moment out of time when all these thoughts raced through her mind. The creature had been looking at her when it bounded out of the ceiling, but now, its focus was totally on Nick in the doorway.

She recognized what was about to happen. They were going to face off, and she was caught right in the middle. Damn. Sal had to figure a way to get out of the way and maybe help, if she could.

Her gun was in her bag, across the room. She had been so discombobulated when she went to bed that she hadn't taken precautions. Fat lot of good that gun did her now, when she couldn't get to it.

All of a sudden, the staring contest ended. The beast leapt for Nick, and he…he changed.

Oh, my stars. He changed. Growing bigger and taller, furrier but not like the other one. Nick's face transformed to something flatter than the snout the other creature sported. And his furry bits were spotted, like a leopard or something.

His clothes shredded as his muscles ripped through the flimsy cloth. It hung off him in strips but didn't seem to hinder his movements at all. She looked at Nick's opponent and realized he too, had strips of cloth around his middle, hanging to about mid-knee as if he'd been wearing pants that hadn't been able to withstand the change from human to…whatever this was.

Sal curled up against the headboard of the bed, trying to make herself as small as possible while the titans clashed in the space between her bed and the doorway. If she could just scoot around them, she might be able to get out of the room.

And then, what? She had no idea, but anything had to be better than being stuck in an enclosed space with a violent fight going on between two massive creatures that were not part of the world she knew.

She would think she was having a nightmare, but this was

all too real. No need to pinch herself. She knew she was awake…and seeing things that just didn't make sense.

Although… She remembered seeing something a few weeks ago. That kid in the parking lot had turned into a cat. She'd thought, at the time, that somebody might have spiked the single drink she had allowed herself at the party. She had to have been seeing things, right?

But the kid had sprouted fur and spots a lot like Nick's before he'd gone all the way to big cat form. He'd been a lot smaller than Nick, of course. He was only a teenager, after all. But what if Nick and the kid were the same?

And what about the werewolf-like thing he was fighting? What had happened to her nice, sane world? Had everyone gone crazy? Or was it just her?

She had to get out of there. Seeing an opening, she scooted, as fast as she could, for the door. She heard all kinds of crashing noises from the room behind her as she ran into the hallway, and her mind blanked. Where could she go? Could she even contemplate leaving Nick alone with that thing?

It occurred to her that Nick was also some kind of creature at the moment, but to her mind, he was still Nick. Still her friend. Still the guy she'd jumped on the sofa a few hours ago. And if he hadn't had the presence of mind and willpower to stop her, she would have had him in bed with her a few minutes ago instead of ready for action.

He'd been right to stop. Harsh as it was to admit. He'd been right.

She ran into the living room and wondered what she could do to help Nick. She spotted his cell phone lying on the table near the balcony doors and ran for it. The noise was pretty intense, so she opened the glass slider and went onto the balcony where it was quieter, tapping the phone to try and find Linelli's number.

She couldn't call the cops. She'd figured that out right away. Normal law enforcement wouldn't know what to do with this situation and would probably only make things worse. But Linelli and Halibut Security had to know something, right? Maybe? It was worth a shot.

She had found the right number and was about to hit *send* when a gust of wind, in the otherwise still night, made her look up. A giant—incredibly giant—bird looked like it was about to land on the balcony.

If she was a weaker woman, Sal would have fainted right then and there. But the bird transformed even as it landed, scrawny bird legs turning into muscular human legs and feathered wings turning into arms. The beak disappeared between one breath and the next, and Collin Hastings' face appeared.

"You're one of them, too?" she whispered, even as he reached behind the big planter and grabbed a kit bag.

"Stay here," he practically barked at her on his way into the condo—heading toward the ongoing confrontation.

He was Nick's friend. He would help Nick, she told herself. Relief went through her, even as the questions bounced through her mind.

The feral werewolf was a tough son of a bitch, but once Sal had gotten clear, Nick was free to use all his moves, without fear of having her caught in the middle of the fight. Smart mate, making room for him to do his thing. He'd stroke her later for being such a good partner.

In his battle form, the cat was much more prevalent in his thoughts. Petting his mate was uppermost in his mind, even as he defeated the feral wolf, knocking him to the carpet, unconscious.

Hasting arrived a second or two late, but still in time to see the wolf sprawl at Nick's feet.

"Where's Sal?" Nick asked, his sharper teeth getting in the way.

The cat wanted to come out and complete the shift, but Nick couldn't do that just now. He had to be human to take care of his mate, and the cat understood, receding quietly as Nick let go of the in-between battle form.

"I told her to stay on the balcony. She saw me shift," he added almost apologetically.

Nick sighed. "Yeah, she saw this, too, so the cat's already out of the bag. I'll square it."

"Let me check in with my team. He shouldn't have been able to get this far. Somebody better be bleeding or they soon will be." Hastings' brows lowered in anger as he started pulling equipment, and clothing, from his kit bag.

Nick knew the hawk shifter would watch over their prisoner, so he turned to leave the room, intending to check on Sal. Only, she was already back in the open doorway, looking around at the wreckage. A lot of the furniture would have to be replaced.

He turned again to meet her gaze and found curiosity more than anything else in her eyes. Maybe this wasn't going to be as bad as he thought.

"You're like that valet kid. A skinwalker, right?" Sal found it hard to keep her thoughts to herself and her mind had just about been blown by what she'd seen. She needed answers. She needed to know.

"A what?" Nick asked, scowling.

"Like the legends of the Navajo. My mother's people," she went on.

"Your mother is Navajo?" Nick seemed surprised.

"Part, anyway. But she wants nothing to do with that side of her heritage. I've done some research, though. I've read about skinwalkers. Is that what you are?"

Nick shook his head. "We call ourselves shifters, or some groups like to call themselves were. Like werewolves. Though we're all shifters, when it comes right down to it."

"Shapeshifters? That's the name you prefer?" She wanted to at least get the terminology straight if she was going to deal with these people.

Nick nodded. "I'm part of the Jaguar Clan, which you probably saw."

"Jaguar." It was starting to make sense. "Like that kid in

the parking lot. I thought I was seeing things, but I wasn't. He's like you."

"One of the junior members of my Clan. He got in trouble for letting you see him," Nick admitted

The man on the floor twitched, drawing her attention.

"I thought maybe somebody had spiked my margarita at the party."

"We thought you might have video," Nick whispered, coming closer.

Hastings was on the phone a few feet away, but he might as well have been on the moon. Sal's full attention was on Nick and their weird conversation.

"Video?" She was genuinely confused.

"The kids said you were holding your phone when they finally spotted you," he told her.

"Oh. No, I wasn't taking pictures. I was just checking the time."

"Well, that's good." Nick sounded relieved. "At least something is going right tonight. There's a lot more we have to discuss, but we can't talk about it just yet. I've got to get him taken care of first," he told her, gesturing toward the man on the floor. He'd reverted to human form now that he was unconscious. If she hadn't seen him a few minutes ago, she would never have known about his animal side. "Just remember," Nick went on. "This conversation isn't over. Merely postponed."

She wasn't sure she liked the sound of that, but he was right. There was still a lot to resolve here. The bad guy was unconscious, but he would come around eventually. Things had to be decided before that happened.

Sal shouldn't have worried about what to do with the werewolf stalker, she realized a few minutes later. Collin Hastings and his people easily took charge of the unconscious man. She trusted that they would know best what to do with a guy who could turn into a *freaking werewolf.* She still couldn't quite get a handle on what she'd seen.

Watching the teenager turn into a big cat to avoid getting

hit by a car had been one thing. That poor boy had looked more frightened of her than anything else when he realized she'd seen everything. He'd scurried away as if his tail was on fire.

What had just happened had been way scarier. Way more dangerous, too. The lunatic had been gunning for her, and if not for Nick's intervention... Well, she hated to think what would have happened to her without Nick and his extra special magical skill set.

"A couple of my people are down, but I have enough on call to mop up without getting the humans involved," Hastings said to Nick after he shut off his cell phone.

"Aren't you going to tie him up or something?" Sal asked, watching the man on the floor. He was starting to show signs of life, and she feared he'd wake up and start fighting again.

"Conventional restraints don't really work that well on our kind," Hastings said in a no-nonsense tone of voice. "But don't worry. We've got this. He won't bother you again."

"What are you going to do with him?" she asked, unable to halt her curiosity.

"That depends," Nick said, entering the conversation.

"On what?" she whispered, looking at Nick. His arms were bare, his clothing in tatters around him, but he still had a rough dignity that nothing could shatter.

"It depends on what he has to say for himself," Nick replied, looking not at her, but at the man on the ground. Sal gazed at him and found herself captured by those swirly yellow eyes. He was awake! "No shifting, pal, or I'll just knock you out again." A growl sounded from the man's throat, and it didn't sound friendly. "Now, do you want to tell us why you're so eager to get to Miss Lane here? So eager that you'd expose the shifter secret to a human?"

"She's not," the man whispered. His voice sounded as if his throat was raw. "She's a witch. Like the bitch who put this spell on me!" The last part came out as a roar, and Hastings grabbed the guy from behind before he could launch himself at Nick again.

Sal started to shake. She was not like her mother. She didn't have that same deadly, dangerous magic.

"Let me understand this," Nick went on reasonably, as if the man hadn't been threatening renewed violence. "Someone put a spell on you, and you think Miss Lane can undo it?" When the man didn't respond, Nick kept talking. "What kind of spell, friend? What did they do to you?" His voice was gentle now, and the man seemed to respond to the kind tone.

"Can't shift all the way. Get stuck in battle form. Hurts," he panted, and even Sal could see the man was in near constant pain. "Makes my wolf crazy."

"I don't doubt it," Nick said understandingly. "What's your name, friend? What Pack do you come from?"

"Tony Gatling from the Sacramento Pack," he replied, sounding a little bit steadier. "I need a witch. Someone who can reverse the spell."

"I hear you, Tony," Nick replied. "But I don't quite agree with the way you've gone about this. We can get you to the Lords and the High Priestess can set you right. If she can't, nobody can."

"The High Priestess? Would she bother herself with the likes of me? I'm not an Alpha," Tony said in a sad voice.

"How long has this been going on, Tony?" Hastings asked, easing the hold on Tony's arms.

"About three months now. I could handle it at first, but as time goes on, my wolf is…" he trailed off.

"Full moon is tomorrow," Hastings mused, sharing a significant look with Nick. Both men had grim expressions.

"If you weren't Alpha before, Tony, your wolf and you have been through hell these past three months. I'd say, for you to have survived that ordeal and still be sane enough at the moment to talk about it with us, you've had a change in dominance." Nick's tone was strong, imparting some of his natural willpower to the disheveled man.

"I left my home Pack when I thought I was getting too dangerous. Thought I'd die somewhere in the desert, but the wolf saw her and made me follow," Tony explained. "I'm sorry if I scared you," he said directly to Sal. "But I need your magic."

"I don't have magic," she told him, feeling sorry about that for the first time in her life. "If I did, I would help you, if I could. I'm so sorry."

The man just looked confused, though the glow in his eyes calmed quite a bit.

"Don't fret, Tony. We're going to get you help. I promise," Nick told him.

"Why would you help me?" Tony sounded miserable now, and it struck Sal's heart, even though the guy had scared her half to death with his antics.

"Because, even though our animals are different, we're all brothers under the skin," Nick said. "Helping you is the right thing to do."

"Who are you?" Tony asked, sounding hopeful for the first time.

"Nick Balam, beta of the Jaguar Clan. And this is Collin Hastings."

"The werehawk investigator," Tony said, turning to look at Hastings. "I've heard of you." His eyes went swirly again, and the moment of sanity faded, but he was calmer now.

"Come on, Tony," Hastings said to the man, walking him toward the door to the bedroom. "I promise you, we'll get you to the High Priestess before the moon rises. Your wolf will run again. Tonight."

Sal could hear Tony weeping as he and Hastings walked down the hall.

CHAPTER 9

Nick did a quick visual survey of the room and shook his head. "Well, you can't stay here. This place is trashed. Sorry." He turned to meet her gaze, almost afraid of what he might see there. Would she be afraid of him now?

"Is it really over?" she whispered, seeming to crumble a bit now that the danger was over.

Nick put a supportive arm around her shoulders. "You're still Sullivan Lane, Hollywood's latest *it* girl. You still need protection. And Hastings will be debriefing Tony. He'll let us know for certain if Tony was behind all the…uh…threatening things found on your property lately." He meant the dead squirrels but didn't want to say it out loud, considering she might be in a fragile state now that the immediate danger had passed.

"It has to be him, doesn't it?" she asked in a shaky voice. "I mean, dead squirrels… Wolves… It makes sense, right? Dogs chase squirrels all the time."

"I'll go out on a limb and say that I believe Tony was most likely responsible, but Hastings will get confirmation for us, just to tie it all up in a nice little bow."

She was trembling, but she also wasn't leaning on him as much as he'd expected. His woman was strong.

"So, what now? I still don't want to go back to that rented

mansion. It was way too big for me anyway."

"And you can't stay in this room. I'll have to arrange for repairs before the rental term is up." He looked around again at the destruction. Damn. This was going to be expensive.

"I think I'd like to camp out on the couch for now and try to calm down. I'm not sure I'll be able to go back to sleep," she said, turning her head toward the door.

He took her cue and let go. She reached for a pillow off the bed and a blanket that had somehow made it through the fight unscathed. Rolling them into a big ball she could carry in her arms, she made her way out to the living room. Nick followed, wondering how she would integrate the things she had learned tonight with her established beliefs about the world. He suspected she'd have a bunch of questions for him about shapeshifters once she had time to settle down and think.

Sal went into the living room and set herself up on the couch. Pillow, blanket and the remote control for the TV, in case she wanted it. All she needed now was a little peace of mind. And maybe a cup of tea. She turned to the kitchen area and found that Nick was already there, putting the kettle on the stove.

"You're a mind reader, too?" she asked, chiding him.

"Knowing your fondness for tea, I thought it was only appropriate to make a pot," he replied, sending her a smile that settled her nerves just the tiniest bit.

No matter if he had turned into a furry, scary, even-bigger-than-he-was-right-now beast, he was still the man she had come to know over the past days. Still Nick. Nice guy and protector of silly starlets.

Foregoing the couch, she went to the island and sat on one of the high chairs, facing toward the kitchen. She needed to talk to him. There were things that needed to be said. Things she wanted to find out.

"Is it really safe to stay here? I mean, nobody else is going to come flying out of the ceiling, right?" She had to know that first and foremost.

"I can assure you, that was a one-off. Now that we're aware of the vulnerability, Hastings has extra operatives in those key spots, and our check-in schedule has been tripled. We're also installing a bunch of sensors in the air ducts. Someone will be along in about twenty minutes with state-of-the-art hardware, and I'll oversee installation. Nobody will have time to crawl through the ventilation system, even if they get past Hastings' people. I'm just sorry I didn't consider entry through the ventilation system a real possibility before. That guy had to be pretty desperate to crawl through such a tight space. Someone my size would never have made it through there."

Nick shook his head as he took a blue and white teapot down from a high shelf. He rinsed it out with hot water from the tap and went about preparing to make the tea while the water heated on the stove.

"But," he went on, "we can relocate anytime you want. In fact, I think we should probably discuss some options in regard to that very topic."

"Options?" she repeated. Her brain wasn't quite up to speed just yet. The shock was still making her jumpy and a little unfocused.

"I'd like to propose a short trip out of town to give Hastings a chance to conclude his investigations. Right now, I'm using his people like security guards, but their real specialty is investigating—especially situations involving the hidden world we inhabit as shapeshifters. If we took you out of the picture for a little bit, then Hastings and his people could devote all their energy to checking every last threat against you, to be certain that poor mixed-up werewolf is the only supernatural problem."

"I suppose I see the wisdom in that, but where would I go, and who would provide the extra special security I might need if that guy wasn't the only one? I don't really feel safe on my own right now," she admitted.

"You wouldn't be on your own," Nick was quick to assure

her. "You'd be with me and my entire Clan. I have just the spot for a little rest and relaxation. It's a private island. All arrivals are under tight control, and the natural defenses and terrain guarantee privacy. Nobody goes there without express permission of the leader of my Clan, who also happens to be my best friend."

"Mark Pepard?" she asked, noting the surprise on his face with satisfaction. "I heard you mention him to Collin Hastings. I wasn't trying to eavesdrop, but that name caught my attention. I didn't realize you were friends with one of the richest men in the world. Which made me wonder why you were working here, on my dinky little security team." She gave him a suspicious look.

He chuckled as the water boiled, and he set about making the tea. Not the reaction she'd expected, but she continued to watch him closely.

"First of all, Halibut Security is not dinky. I'm very happy for my human friends who own the company and proud of their success. They really are the best of the best, and you did the right thing hiring them over their competitors. If this had been a normal situation, their people would have been perfect for the job."

"But this wasn't normal. This was…magical." She said the word with all the horror she had built up over the years of seeing her mother's rogue magic and the way it had torn her little family apart. Nick gave her a questioning look, but she wasn't talking about that. Not yet. Not ever, if she could help it.

"Yeah, somehow, that poor guy thought you were the answer to his problem. I'm still not sure why, but he was as close to feral as I've seen anyone go, without losing it completely. Who knows what was going on in his confused mind?" Nick set the teapot down in the center of the island then placed a mug in front of each of their places before taking his own seat across from her.

He poured them both steaming mugs of the tea, and she enjoyed the quiet moment to collect her thoughts. On some level, she was aware that she was moving and thinking more slowly than usual. Must be the shock of what had happened, but at least she was still functioning, and starting to feel steadier with each passing minute.

"Stop me if I'm wrong, but I get the feeling you came here to check up on me, right? After I saw the valet kid turn into a leopard?" Her tone was accusatory, but it didn't seem to faze him at all.

"Jaguar," he corrected, gently. "I know we all have spots, but jaguars are native to the Americas. Leopards had a different evolution and stick mostly to their own territories, in other parts of the world."

"So, there are...were-leopards, too?" She almost held her breath waiting for his answer.

"Yep. Pretty much all the major predatory species have a shifter equivalent, with a few exceptions, of course. But there aren't as many of us as you might be imagining. We're still pretty rare." He sipped his tea as if this was a normal conversation while her mind was blown all over again. This was a night for revelations, it seemed.

"You came here to check me out. To see if I would spill the beans. Or to find out if I had pictures or video of that kid. Am I right?"

She couldn't help it. She felt abused by the fact that he'd had ulterior motives the whole time he'd been with her. She'd thought they were friends, and really, he'd been spying on her. Probably searching her house and going through her stuff, too.

Nick didn't seem the least bit embarrassed. He touched his finger to his nose and nodded. A silly gesture that probably should have made her grin, but she just wasn't in the mood. She felt a little betrayed.

"I'm head of security for my Clan. If one of our kids messed up enough to let a human see him shift, in public, then I had to make sure what that human would do with such information. We live in secret. For hundreds of years, all shifters everywhere have agreed to keep the secret. It's just safer for us that way, though in the distant past, people knew about us."

"All those South American legends about jaguar gods?" she ventured, earning a big smile from him.

"Yeah, some of our ancestors might have taken advantage on occasion, though my understanding is that they were mostly benevolent to the people they ruled over. At least, I hope they were. It was all a long time ago, and nobody living now was alive back then, so all we have are stories that were handed down over the generations." Nick sipped his tea, giving her time to let that sink in.

"Well, I'm not going to blab about what I saw. Your secret is safe with me, and no, I don't have any photos, or video, or hard evidence of any kind. Frankly, until an hour ago, I thought I'd been hallucinating anyway."

"That's reassuring, but, Sal, although I may have initially come here to check up on you, somewhere along the line, my motives changed." His voice had dropped to an intimate growl. Her midsection clenched, responding to the intent look in his eyes. *Oh, boy.*

She had to clear her throat before speaking again. "Um…how so?"

"I didn't want to stop before," he admitted, her brain knowing exactly what he meant, even if the change in topic was rapid. "Hastings was on the balcony, flapping his damned wings, reminding me of my purpose here. Otherwise, I would've done everything in my power to convince you to spend the night with me. I'm very attracted to you, on pretty much every level." The admission in that low, compelling voice was making her insides do a little squirmy dance, but he wasn't done. "I've never spent much time in this town or around movie people. You proved, right away, that all my half-formed expectations were wrong. You're amazing, Sal. You're kind, generous, funny and smart. You're not an empty-headed actress who only cares about her hair and clothes. I have to apologize for my misconceptions."

Sal liked his honesty. "No need. I know a lot of women in

this town who are like that. Lucky for you, I'm not one of them."

"Indeed, you are not." His voice got a little growly, and rather than frighten her, it made her hot. "You are completely unique in my experience, and I'm giving you fair warning, I would like to court you."

"*Court* me?" She tilted her head at the old-fashioned word. "Like, you want to date?"

He nodded. "More than date, actually. I'd like to take you home to meet my Alpha, and hope you'll consider beginning a relationship with me."

Hmm. He certainly couldn't make it clearer than that.

"Is meeting your Alpha like when humans meet the parents?" she wanted to know.

He chuckled. "You'll meet my parents, too. They recently moved to the island and have taken it as an opportunity to butt into my life again. But I don't really mind. It's good to see them happy and safe." He paused a moment, a faint smile on his face, thinking of his folks. She liked that. "In my case, meeting my Alpha means meeting my best friend. After all, he's the one who sent me here, so in a way, I have him to thank for meeting you."

"He's on this island you're talking about? The private island where I'll be safe from any stalkers that might remain while Collin Hastings lets his people loose on my case?"

"Exactly." Nick nodded again, as if in approval of her summation of the situation. "You could probably make something of the trip if you want to talk to your PR people. Mark is well known, and his movements are watched almost constantly. We've become pretty adept at feeding the press enough information to keep them busy while going about our business. You could explain the sudden change in your schedule by saying you'd received an unexpected invitation from Mark and his new wife to visit them. No press is allowed on or near the island, so once you get there, you'll be completely safe and out of the public eye."

"That kind of sounds like heaven right about now," she

admitted. "I still haven't gotten used to the paparazzi. I probably never will. I honestly never expected this level of success for my acting career. I was content just to be making a living, but fame sort of snuck up on me, and now, I'm stuck with it."

Nick was nodding understandingly. "Same thing happened to Mark, though his fame is from the money and the business success. The man just has a golden touch, which is good for our Clan, of course, but he's also a great guy and a strong Alpha. As his unexpected fame grew, we had to come up with ways to negotiate the minefield of the press and still keep our secrets. It hasn't always been easy, but over the years, we've come up with some sound strategies. I'd be happy to share some of our tricks, if you want."

"Yeah, I'd like that." She was beginning to thaw a bit on the whole spying thing, but she wanted to know more about his animal side and his people. "Nick, can I ask you something about being a shapeshifter? I mean, now that I know, there's no way to un-know it, right? So, would you mind just clarifying a couple of things for me?"

Nick's expression grew serious, but she couldn't tell exactly what that meant. Was he concerned that she wanted to know more? Or was he pleased? She couldn't quite tell.

"Go ahead. I'll tell you if there's anything I can't answer." His words didn't give her any further clues as to how he was taking her interest, so she just forged ahead.

"Well, that guy, Tony, said something about being stuck in battle form? What's that all about?" She figured she'd start there, but in truth, she wanted to know everything.

"Battle form is the half-way state between human and animal. Young warriors train to hold the shift right there, in the middle, because that form is bigger, stronger and fiercer than either of the alternatives. Only strong people can hold the shift. It's not something everyone can do. Alphas and the more dominant shifters can do it more easily than others, but submissive shifters can't really do it at all. They just go from human to their animal, no real pause in between."

"That's why you told him his standing might have changed, right? The fact that he's been forced to hold the battle form for so long and managed to stay somewhat sane—though I guess I'm using that term loosely—means he's stronger than he thought," she reasoned.

"Yep. If the people we sent him to can fix him up—and if they can't, no one can—then I suspect his rank in his Pack hierarchy will have changed quite a bit. I'm still wondering why he pegged you for a witch, though. Have you ever dabbled in magic or maybe played a role in a movie he might have misconstrued?" Nick asked, turning the tables on her.

What could she tell him? She never spoke of her mother. Not to anyone. But she knew Nick's shapeshifting secret now. Should she trust him?

She had to think about it a bit more. She couldn't make such an important decision when she was so off-balance like this.

"None of my roles have had anything like that," she hedged and did her best to change the subject. "When you change, do you still retain your personality and thoughts or is the human half hidden while the beast takes over?"

"That's a good question."

He looked like he knew she was redirecting him, but was willing to play along for now. The man was really a lot smarter than he let on, but she was starting to be able to read his body language and expressions. Her instincts told her that he would come back to the topic again...eventually.

"Yes, we're still in control when we shift. I'm still the same me, with the same knowledge and reasoning ability when I'm in my fur. Just like the cat is always present in my human form. We are one and the same. Indivisible, though sometimes, we speak of our different forms as if they're separate entities. They're really not. We're still who we are, regardless of what shape we wear." His expression tightened as he went on. "There are some circumstances where a shifter can go feral—our version of insanity, when the animal takes over completely and isn't quite right in the head. Tony had moments of lucidity, but I suspect most of the time he was teetering on the wrong side of the edge. Hopefully, we got to him in time, and he'll be able to be rehabilitated."

"Does that sort of thing happen a lot?"

"No, not really, though we do have enemies. Tony must've run afoul of a mage who'd gone over to the dark side." He grimaced again.

"Mage? Like a witch or wizard? I thought they were all evil. That magic caused you to do evil things."

He looked at her sharply, and she wondered if she'd said too much. Probably, but it looked like he wasn't going to call her on it just yet.

"Magic is neither inherently good nor is it evil. It's what we choose to do with it that is the deciding factor. That's where free will comes in. There are many mages working on the side of Light, fighting against evil wherever they find it. Most shifters do the same, though there are the occasional bad apples, as in any culture or group."

She frowned, inwardly rejecting his words. He was implying her mother had *chosen* to do evil things when the magic came upon her. That couldn't be true. It just couldn't.

But maybe... Maybe she was having the same kind of problem as Tony. Maybe someone had deliberately done something to her.

It was all pretty far-fetched and went against what Sal had thought most of her life, but she was learning all sorts of new things since she saw that valet kid shift and Nick had come into her life. She couldn't come right out and ask. She'd have to reveal too much. But she could stick close to Nick, go to the island and meet more of his people. Maybe she could pick something up that might give her more answers.

And she'd be with Nick. The man attracted her on every level and made her lady parts stand up and take notice in a way they hadn't done in a long, long time...if ever. She wanted to spend more time with him, despite what she'd seen.

Somehow—and here, she was trusting her instincts

again—she just knew that he would never use his strength against her. He would never hurt her. On the contrary, he would protect her in every way while she was with him. She knew that like she knew her own heart. He was definitely one of the good guys. A scary, furry good guy but definitely a good guy.

"I think I'd like to go to your island, at least while Mr. Hastings and his people are doing their work. Unfortunately, I can't just disappear. I'll have to clear it with my manager and the PR folks, but I think it'll work out. If your friend Mark is amenable, a leaked story that I've been given an exclusive invite to Pepard's private island ought to settle any negative speculation in the tabloids. They'll love that story and start wondering how I'm connected with Pepard, which I certainly don't mind. I just hope he doesn't."

"Mark is newly married, so we can always say he invited his new wife's favorite actress over as a surprise for his new bride," Nick offered.

"Oh, that could work," she told him, grinning at him as her mind sorted through the story. It really was a good one that would save them any romantic speculation about her and Pepard. It would make the billionaire look like a hero of romantic gestures. "I'll make the calls in the morning, as soon as everyone is in the office. How soon can we leave?"

"As soon as you like. I have a private jet at the airport."

"You do?" She looked at him with wide eyes. This man was full of surprises.

"I can fly it, too, though I won't have to do all the work. A couple of younger Clan members came with me and are using the downtime to see the sights while I'm on this mission," he told her. "Both are pilots and will share the flying time with me so we can do a straight hop, though we'll need to set down and refuel at some point, since we'll be crossing the whole country."

They talked about the island and their plans as the night matured into pre-dawn. Sal calmed visibly as their conversation wore on and Nick told her about the mansion on the island. He'd have her stay there until she was ready to accept more. The mansion was a relic of the previous owner—a human with no awareness of the magical world all around him. It was set upslope from the only decent place to land a boat on the island.

A dormant volcano, the island had sheer cliffs around much of its base that made it next to impossible to come in by sea from any other direction than the small sandy shore below the mansion. Up in the jungle, hidden from prying eyes and even satellites, was what would become the real settlement on Jaguar Island. Surrounded on three sides by inward-arching cliff faces, the ancient caldera would house new community buildings and individual residences for any member of the Jaguar Clan who wanted to live there.

It was a place where they hoped to rebuild what was once a thriving population. Jaguar shifters would be safe there, to live and grow, have children and shapeshift if the mood struck, without having to worry about being seen by anyone who wasn't a Clan member. It would be paradise, and Nick sincerely hoped Sal would find it to her liking.

With any luck, and if the Goddess was smiling down on them, he'd be able to declare his love at some point very soon and convince her to be his mate. If she had been a shifter, she would have known as soon as he had—maybe even sooner— that they were meant to be together. But she was human, and she had to be wooed.

He would do that by showing her what his life was like. He'd introduce her to Mark, his folks, and the other members of the Clan. They would love her, and he hoped she would enjoy meeting them, as well. They would help him show her what it was like to be a member of a shifter Clan. They would help him convince her that Nick could protect her for the rest of her life.

He hadn't done too well so far, but then, he hadn't been expecting trouble of a magical variety. Still, he would do his utmost to be the best mate possible, including protecting her from every possible thing that might come her way in the future.

CHAPTER 10

The jet and private terminal were both opulent and a bit overwhelming. Nick had introduced her to two other Clan members, as he called them. A bright-eyed young woman named Lucinda and a man named Keith, who was close enough in looks to be her twin but was, in fact, her younger brother.

The brother and sister team took the controls for the first part of the flight, getting them into the air and headed for the east coast. Nick kept Sal company in the small cabin, showing her where they kept the snacks and drinks.

"We can get lunch on the ground when we set down for fuel," Nick told her.

He raised his voice only slightly to be heard over the noise of the engine. The cabin must be heavily insulated against the high-pitched sound of the jet engine that was mounted to the back of the small plane.

"There's a great steak place near the little airport we use in Texas that will deliver out to the terminal. I always try to stop there when I'm in the area," he went on.

They talked of his travels and the work he did for, and with, Mark Pepard. The conversation was light in nature, which suited her just fine. The last few weeks had been very trying on her nerves, and the revelations of the past hours had been the most jarring of all. She would need some time to assimilate all the new information he had given her about the world.

How could she not have known—or even suspected—that things like shapeshifters could actually exist? With all the weirdness in her own family, it seemed strange that she had never even considered it before.

At least she knew now. That was something. Most people probably lived their entire lives never even considering that some of the ancient folk tales about werewolves and magic might possibly be true.

When they set down in Texas, Sal put on the baseball cap and big sunglasses Nick handed her before exiting the plane. She wasn't really trying to hide her identity, but she also didn't want to draw too much attention. As promised, Nick ordered lunch for all of them from the steak house he favored, and they waited in the small private terminal for the delivery while Lucinda and Keith saw to the refueling.

When a handsome young man with the big bag of takeout arrived some minutes later, Nick greeted him as an old friend. Apparently, they were on a first-name basis, and Nick took the time to introduce her to the much younger male named Kevin.

"We're able to talk freely here," Nick told her in confidential tones. "Big Wolf Airport is run by Kevin's dad, the Alpha of the Big Wolf Ranch Pack, which owns the ranch and airport that bears its name. The staff are all Pack members, and when we set down, we received the code that said no non-shifters were here right now. The airport is open to the public, of course, but there are bigger and better-situated air strips closer to the cities that most humans prefer unless they're doing cross-country flights like we are."

"Shifters own all this?" Sal asked, impressed.

"And the steak house, too," Nick agreed, nodding and smiling at Kevin. "How's your family been since the last time I was through?"

"We're all good, sir, though my older sister is driving

everybody crazy, but what else is new?" Kevin rolled his eyes, and both men smiled.

"Give them my best, and thanks for bringing this out," Nick said, handing over a wad of bills to the young man. "Keep the change," he said magnanimously, when Kevin tried to give some of it back.

"Just wanted to say I really liked your last movie," Kevin said, turning unexpectedly to look at Sal. She was a little floored to think that she might actually have fans among shapeshifters.

"Thanks," she replied, giving the youngster a pleased smile, which made his cheeks flush a bit. Right then and there, Kevin endeared himself to her forevermore.

He was an adolescent kid, just like so many others she'd met since her movie made it big, and they'd all had similar reactions. He was adorable. Even if he could turn into some sort of predator—she was betting a wolf, based on the name of the airport. A *big* one, if the people lived up to the name of their Pack.

"Wanna take a selfie?" she asked on impulse. She'd learned recently that pushy folks would ask, but the shy ones were reticent.

The kid's face lit up, and he reached for his phone with eager fingers, pushing buttons to set it up to take the photo. Then, he turned to Nick, and Sal figured he was going to ask if Nick would take the photo, but his words surprised her.

"Would you be in it, too, sir?" Kevin's tone was hesitant, but still eager.

"Sure," Nick said easily, moving closer to wrap his arm around the younger man's shoulders on one side while Sal framed Kevin on the other. She took the phone and snapped the picture, taking another, just for insurance, in case somebody was blinking. Then, she handed the phone back to Kevin.

"This is so awesome. Thanks!" He was tapping on his phone to check the images. "Now, I have proof I got to talk with Nick Balam and Sullivan Lane on the same day. My sister's going to kick herself for not wanting to do the airport run today."

The kid walked away, all smiles, and Sal had to wonder at Nick's level of celebrity among his own kind. It sure sounded like the selfie with Nick was more important than the fact that she was in it, too. She didn't mind, of course, but it was a turnaround from the way things had been of late.

"You're famous among your people, aren't you?" she asked him with a sly grin as they walked through the small terminal, heading back toward the jet.

He shrugged, seeming a little uncomfortable with the topic. "My Alpha is the famous one. Mark goes all over the world, and I go with him. Occasionally, I end up on the front page of the paper in the background of something Mark is doing, but nobody outside shifter circles really knows who I am. I like to keep it that way."

"But among shifters…?" she insisted.

"Well, I am a pretty visible Beta to Mark's Alpha," he allowed. "And most other shifter groups have slightly different power structures than the Jaguar Clan. The Alpha is like our political leader. I'm his right hand and head of security. He leads. I protect. Though, to be fair, Mark is a great protector, as well. Our forefathers just set up this hierarchy to suit our independent natures. A wolf Pack functions a lot differently, but they probably don't know enough about our inner workings to realize just how different we are."

"Cats and dogs," she whispered, hoping her words would only reach Nick. She didn't want to inadvertently insult anybody from the wolf Pack.

Nick laughed aloud at her words, sending her a smile. "Yeah, it's evolution, I guess. There's a reason we're a Clan and they're a Pack. They're a lot more involved with each other's lives than cats would tolerate, though we're learning to live together in harmony, now that we're settling the island."

She wanted to ask more about that last comment, but

they'd reached the airplane, and everybody was ready to go. Nick ate dinner with her while the brother and sister team got them back into the air. When Nick was finished eating, he went up to the cockpit and sent the other two back one at a time to eat their meals.

Sal talked a bit with them both, but they were trying to eat, and she didn't really want to make them talk, so she looked out the window and got comfortable. The next thing she knew, she was waking up after a deep doze. The plane was noticeably pitched forward, and Nick was sitting to her left.

"Are we landing already?" she asked, surprised at how groggy she was. She must've been sleepier than she'd thought.

"Yeah. We'll be on the ground in a few minutes. If you look out, you'll probably get a good view of the island once we're through the clouds," he told her.

She looked out, shaking off her lethargy. She wanted to see this island he'd told her about.

Sal wasn't disappointed with her first vision of Jaguar Island. It was a craggy mountain sticking up out of the sea. Covered in jungle, it was an emerald jewel set in an azure ocean. And it looked just as forbidding as it did magical.

She could see the slopes of the ancient volcano, just under the froth of greenery as they grew closer. A white sandy beach showed on just one side of the island, the rest being made up of sheer drop offs to the sea. There was a dock and a small airstrip below a giant, classically-styled mansion that sat a short distance up the side of the slope that was gentlest on this side of the island.

The brother-sister pilot team set them down gently and then taxied the jet a short distance toward a large hangar that housed several other planes of all shapes and sizes. Jets. Prop planes. She could even see a seaplane bobbing in the water, tied to a nearby dock.

Something about the place made her tingle. As the jet rolled to a stop, she felt something building inside, and anxiety began to roil in the pit of her stomach.

"I don't know about this," she murmured to herself, but

of course, Nick heard.

He turned back to look at her, stopping what he was doing to give her a questioning look.

"Are you all right? I promise, nobody here will harm you. Far from it."

Nick looked so earnest, she wanted to believe him, but the feeling inside wasn't going away. In fact, it was increasing.

"I'm sorry, Nick. I really am. I'm just not sure I can go through with this." Panic began to set in as a sensation of dread filled her.

"There's nothing to fear. I promise you." He tried again, letting the cabin crew depart ahead of them with a single nod. It was just Nick and Sal left on the jet, the cabin door open, letting in a humid, flower-scented breeze.

Sal felt tears gather behind her eyes. There was no way out. She felt something rising that would not be held back, and she dreaded the idea that it might be the heritage she never wanted to acknowledge. Though she had suppressed it all her life, she recognized the sensations of magic.

"I'm so sorry," was all she could say as she felt it rise higher, nearly overwhelming her.

Nick scowled and knelt in front of her seat, reaching for her hands.

"Honey, what's wrong?" he whispered as his hands enfolded hers.

And then, it happened.

Sparks. Visible sparks. Red, yellow, orange, white. Pearlescent motes of magic floating on the air. It started like a mini volcanic explosion originating where their hands met, but it didn't have the destructive power she so greatly feared.

"What the...?" Nick looked at her sharply. "You're a mage?" His accusation held traces of betrayal, and she felt as if he had slapped her, though it was only with words.

She let go of his hands and turned away, tears streaking down her face.

"I have no magic," she said, repeating the mantra that she had used for so many years.

"Lie," he said, his voice harsh. "That was magic, Miss Lane. Even I can see that." His tone was still rough, but he seemed to be moderating a bit as the first shock wore off. "But you're not surprised. You know about magic. How could you know about it if you don't use it? And why are you so deep in denial? Did you hurt someone in the past?"

She shook her head. She never talked about this, but she didn't see a way out without giving him something.

"Not me. I don't have magic," she repeated, knowing it wasn't entirely true.

"Someone close to you, then," Nick said, his tone growing even cagier. She had no idea what was going through his mind. He was impossible to read, just at the moment.

Much as it pained her, she would have to give him the truth. At least, some of it.

"My mother," she whispered. It was hard to break the self-imposed rule she had about never speaking of her mother.

"You mother was a mage?" Nick pushed, relentless.

"A witch. That's what she calls it," Sal confirmed, tears leaking out of her eyes. This was painful to discuss. She'd never thought she'd tell anyone about her mother's problems. She'd never thought anyone could understand.

But Nick might. Maybe.

"Wait a minute. Your mother is alive? All the data I found said that Sullivan Lane was an orphan who had never known her parents." Now, Nick looked angry. At her? Probably. But possibly also at himself for taking her story at face value. She cringed.

"She's locked up in a place for the criminally insane," she admitted in a small voice. "Has been for years. Decades."

"*Criminally* insane?" he repeated, putting emphasis on the first word.

"When the magic takes her, it does…horrible things." She looked into his eyes, seeing the confusion, skepticism and anger there. "I know you think magic isn't good or evil, but you're wrong. My mother isn't evil." She could hear the pleading tone in her own voice.

After a couple of tense moments where he searched her gaze for only he knew what, Nick sat back on his haunches and gave a great sigh. "So, at best, your mother's a rogue mage with no control over her wild magic, and you're in complete denial about your own power and heritage."

"I don't have magic," she repeated her mantra. "I refuse to have magic!"

Her voice got a little shrill, so she clamped down on her escaping emotions, as she had always done. Giving in to strong emotion invited the magic in, which is something Sal refused to do. It wouldn't take her without a fight.

"Why didn't you tell me all this before?" Nick asked quietly.

"I don't talk about my mother. Not ever," she told him. "I wouldn't have said anything now, if not for whatever those sparks were."

"The island is a long-dormant volcano. There's lots and lots of earth magic here. It seems to have an unexpected influence on people with latent magical power. You're not the first to have created unexpected sparks." Nick rubbed his hand over his short hair, a sign of frustration—or perhaps, contemplation. "In fact, maybe they can help sort you out. Honey, you have to realize you can't go on like this. Denial only works to a certain point, and I think you've already left that in the dust." He got off the floor of the plane, moving to sit beside her. "I think I understand now why that poor mixed-up werewolf thought you could help him. He sensed what you've been hiding all this time."

Sal shook her head, not wanting to believe any of it. Magic was evil, and she wanted no part of it.

Right?

Doubt began to creep in. Nick was the first person she'd ever met who she could talk to about magic and all the things that had scared her for so very long. Maybe he was right? Or, at least, maybe he had more information about the entire problem than she did. Maybe he *could* help. Maybe it was time to stop living in fear.

After all, if one werewolf saw magic in her and stalked her because of it, there could be others. She certainly didn't want to deal with this kind of thing on an ongoing basis. Maybe there was a way to stop future problems before they could develop. It was at least worth checking out.

Hesitantly, she came to a decision. She was stuck on this island for now. She didn't even know if they would let her leave after this latest discovery. She might as well see it through and try to learn what she could about her affliction.

"Do you really think they can help me?" Her own voice sounded pitiful in her ears. This was a low point, for sure.

"I'm confident we can help you. The Jaguar Clan might be small, but we're mighty, and we have an in with a very powerful mage who works on the side of Light." Nick winked at her, as if she was supposed to understand what he meant.

"Light? That's the good guys, right? The cowboys with white hats?" She wanted to make sure, not that she was in a position to do anything about it, even if they weren't.

"Most definitely. White hats, all the way. That's the only kind we allow in our territory." He was smiling again, but she sensed a core of steel running through his words. "But I'm warning you, now, Sal, no more omissions. No more lies."

"I wasn't lying," she defended herself. "I just didn't tell you everything. To be fair, you didn't reveal everything to me right away either, did you?"

She could tell by the uncomfortable expression on his face that she had just scored a point. She didn't like the feeling. Sal wasn't one to play games, or feel superior when she won an argument. She was more of a peacemaker, happy when she got along with everyone around her.

This was a tricky situation for her. She was in his territory, totally dependent on him for not only hospitality but transportation, as well. If Nick didn't want to let her off the island, she wasn't getting off the island. Maybe coming here hadn't been such a bright idea after all.

Nick couldn't believe what had just happened. Sal a witch? No fucking way. Lightning didn't strike twice. Not normally.

Mark had just mated a woman who'd had no idea about her magical heritage. Her father was a mage of great power, but William Howell the Fourth and his daughter, Shelly, were the last of a great line of mages. When Shelly had shown no sign of sharing in the family gift, her father had done everything he could to protect her, including distancing himself from his only daughter and keeping her in the dark about magic and her family's past achievements.

When Mark had brought Shelly to Jaguar Island, the ancient volcano had sparked her latent magical power. From what Mark had told Nick, it had come as a complete surprise to Shelly. She hadn't been hiding anything. Shelly truly hadn't known anything about it.

Sal's situation was quite different. She knew about magic. Her mother had been committed, for heaven's sake, due to what sounded like wild, uncontrollable magic. Sal had seen it, Nick had no doubt. She understood how devastating it could be.

He wondered, though, if she had ever seen the good side. Had she ever experienced the wonder of the power she denied? Probably not. The thought made him sad, and determined to help her understand the true nature of magic before she left the island.

That's supposing everything she had just told him was on the level. If she was lying to him, things would be a lot more complicated.

But, first things first. He had to determine the best way to deal with this new situation. He had intended to put her up at the mansion, among all the other jaguars and guests—Shelly's father was staying on the island for a while to teach his daughter about her magic. But that plan seemed like a bad idea with this new development.

Shelly was an architect, and she was busy designing new structures that would eventually become the heart of the Clan's settlement. Right now, though, there was only the mansion that had been built by the non-magical former owner of the island, plus a few outbuildings. Hangars, a warehouse and a boathouse were in this immediate area, around the airstrip and docks. None of them would do. Plus, he didn't want to put her too close to the temptation of the airplanes and boats. If she wanted to escape the island, this is the only place she could do it from.

No, he needed tighter control over her. At least for the time being. Until he figured out whether or not she was truly a threat to him or his people.

The revelations of the past few minutes had knocked him sideways. Nick had been so certain he'd checked her out fully. He'd been so confident that she would be his mate, and therefore, even if she had dark secrets in her past, they would all resolve easily, so they could begin their life together.

He'd been a fool. He'd been around long enough to know that things didn't always work out, and what looked perfectly innocent on the surface could hide the darkest evil underneath. Not that he thought Sal was evil, but the things she had told him had definitely roused his suspicions.

The fact that he'd let down his guard so much as to be surprised was telling. A mistake on his part could spell disaster for not just him, but his Alpha and the Clan as a whole. Nick had to be better than this. He had to put the Clan first. Always. There could be no exceptions.

He'd known this his entire life, but he'd been lulled into incompetence by Sal's presence. Had she done it on purpose? Had she maneuvered him into issuing the invitation into the heart of the Clan's territory?

Goddess! He'd been such a fool. The thought played over and over in his mind. Nick hadn't made such a bad mistake in a very long time, but now, he was stuck. He had to fix this. He had to make the best of the situation. Somehow.

A sudden thought occurred to him. There was a somewhat primitive cabin he had used when first surveying the island. It was on the other side of the volcanic caldera, on the opposite side of the island from the mansion. As far away as they could get and still be on the island.

He'd take her there. He'd stay with her there, away from everybody else, until he figured out exactly what kind of threat she posed. She might not like it, but it was the only alternative that made sense right now.

Nick got up and went to the open door of the jet, flagging down Lucinda, who was doing a walk-around of the plane post-flight. He informed her of his change of plans and asked her to arrange for Sal's luggage to be loaded onto an off-road vehicle. Lucinda looked perplexed, but she didn't ask questions. Nick was the Beta of the Clan. If he wanted to do things a certain way, that was up to him.

CHAPTER 11

"Aren't we going to that big house up there?" Sal asked when Nick had her and her belongings in the four-wheel drive vehicle and was already underway.

The path he was taking didn't look like they were headed toward the mansion on the hill. She didn't see any other options. The jungle canopy was pretty dense. Maybe there were guest accommodations hidden somewhere else among the trees.

Or maybe he was taking her to her doom. Sal mentally kicked herself for not thinking this through. Of course, she should have realized that someone like Nick—a freaking shapeshifter, for heaven's sake—would be able to see through her. She hadn't lied, exactly, but she definitely hadn't been honest with him. Heck, she hadn't been honest with anyone. Ever.

Her mother's fate and Sal's own denial of magic was her deepest, darkest secret. She'd never told anyone before, and she wished she hadn't had to reveal it now. Magic had only ever caused problems for her and her family. Why had she thought it would be any different now?

Foolish, Sal. Really, really foolish.

Fate was playing with her. On the mainland, she might've had some control, but she'd given it all up by agreeing to stay on this private island. She had no way off, until Nick provided one. She was essentially a prisoner—of her own making.

She should have seen it coming, but she'd been distracted by everything that had happened. And, admittedly, by the man. Nick had a way of getting right under her skin and into her mind until all she could think about was him.

Attraction was a mild word to describe her feelings. Obsession was closer to the mark, and it scared her. Put her way off kilter. Made her make foolish decisions.

"No, not yet," Nick finally answered her question after a slight delay. "There's a cabin out a ways that's probably better for our purposes. It's private, and it's well camouflaged. The perfect little hideaway."

What he was describing could as easily be thought of as a prison. A convenient place to hide her until he decided her fate. She might never return from such a place. Or—maybe—it could be just what he described. A private getaway where she could be alone while she figured things out.

He must have seen concern on her face. After glancing at her, he went on.

"I'll call Mark and inform him of our problem. I don't want to expose him or his new bride to rogue magic, just in case the island has more surprises in store for us." He shifted gears and turned onto a steep trail that went almost straight up the slope of the mountain. "This place is highly magical, and it's happened before that the ancient volcano woke a latent magic. Luckily, we have a mage visiting here, right now, who might be able to give us some advice. There's also a wise woman who is part of our Clan. She might be able to help, as well. Once Mark hears your story, he'll send someone to check things out. Never fear."

But fear was her constant companion as they drove the rest of the way to the cabin in silence. Her mind was whirling a mile a minute, but she did her best not to let it show. She tried to resign herself to her fate. What will be will be, she kept reminding herself. She was too far in it now. There was no turning back.

There hadn't been a chance to turn back since they'd left Texas. If only she'd been thinking clearly. If only she'd stopped there to puzzle things through. She could've spent time among the werewolves, maybe, regrouping. Or she could have turned around and went back to California, taking her chances with what would happen next.

Why, oh, why, had she listened to Nick? Was a handsome face and a compelling stare enough to make her lose all common sense? Apparently so, she thought with self-aimed disapproval.

Nick had smiled at her, and she'd lost all touch with her reality. The harsh reality that had told her to stay away—far away—from all things even remotely magical. Nick was a freaking *shapeshifter*, for goodness sake! What had possessed her to think that being around him would be safe?

Nick drove straight to the cabin, his mind working overtime. How had he let her sneak under his defenses? Had he been thinking with his cock and not his brain? Yeah, he admitted to himself in disgust, he definitely had.

The only thing that would have made it worse is if he believed she had done it deliberately. His instincts told him that what she had finally admitted about her past was true. She wasn't lying to him now—though, to be accurate, she hadn't really been *lying* to him in the first place. She'd simply omitted to tell him about certain key facets of her family's history.

If he hadn't been distracted by her beauty and his attraction to her… If he'd been doing his job properly… He should have uncovered the falsehood in her background data. He *should have* been able to discover that not only was her mother alive, but that she was an inmate in a facility for the criminally insane, of all things.

How could he have missed it? That was exactly the kind of thing he excelled at discovering. His skills at investigation, background checks, creating secure perimeters, and good old-fashioned bodyguard work were what had allowed him to rise to the rank of Beta. The fact that he'd screwed up so badly with Sal made him rethink his worthiness for the position.

He was going to have to admit his failing to Mark. It would be well within the Alpha's right to strip Nick of his rank and put someone else in his place. Nick would take his lumps if it meant better security for the Clan. He always put the Clan first.

But it would definitely be a blow—a hard lesson to his ego, and perhaps irreparable damage to his friendship with Mark. Nick hated putting his friend in this position.

They finally pulled up in front of the cabin, and Nick was grateful that he had insisted on keeping the old structure. He'd even sent crews out to renovate and repair the place. It was sound now. Waterproof, as it hadn't been just a few months ago, and equipped with all the modern conveniences a small generator and a supply of fuel could afford.

Some of the security patrols rotated in and out of here on their rounds. If they wanted to patrol in human form, the cabin was always ready to accommodate off-shift sleep periods for the lone cats who prowled the slopes of the mountain.

Nobody was up here right now. Nick had checked before setting out from the airstrip. He'd also put the word out that the cabin would be occupied and should be added to the security rounds. Sal wouldn't be aware of the added eyes watching her, but Nick felt it was important to make up for his oversight. Sal had already fooled him once. He'd be a complete idiot not to seek help in watching her when it was readily available.

He wasn't going to do this without backup. She would probably never know that she was under such close surveillance, but it reassured Nick to know that, even if his judgment was clouded by her presence—or her magic—other jaguars would be watching, ready to leap in if he needed help.

Nick didn't truly think Sal posed any sort of serious threat to the Alpha couple or the Clan as a whole, but he was through taking chances. His judgment where she was concerned had already been proven faulty. He wasn't going to go it alone when he was on Jaguar Island, with the support of the Clan behind him.

He stopped the Jeep in front of the door and shut off the engine. He just sat there for a moment, his hands on top of the steering wheel, his eyes facing forward, staring out at the jungle. Finally, he breathed a deep sigh, allowing the humid air to comfort him. This was his habitat. His home.

"I'm truly sorry about all this," Nick said, not looking at her. "It might only be for a few days. I just want to make sure everything checks out."

"You want to make sure I'm not a danger to your people," she said in a somber tone that made him turn his head to look at her. "I get it," she went on, holding up one hand palm outward toward him. "Magic has turned my life upside down more than once. It's a curse, and I'm sorry to have brought it to your island. That was never my intention. Believe me."

"Honey, you didn't bring it here. Magic is all around us. All the time. It's just more concentrated right here, where the earth energy is still so strong." Nick felt conflicted. His instinct was to comfort her, but he was wary of more unintentional deceit. He really had no way of knowing if she was being completely honest with him, now, and her track record in that area wasn't the greatest.

"I won't pretend to understand it," she told him. "I've never understood it. I've never really wanted to. I've just prayed for it to be gone, but it always comes back and ruins things all over again." She shook her head. "This is the first time it's happened to me, though. Usually, it's my mother who ends up in trouble." He thought he saw a tear roll down her far cheek before she turned away. "I never wanted this, but I guess it's finally caught up with me. My life is over."

Her words hit him hard, causing pain in the region of his heart. She sounded so dejected, so hopeless. It hurt him to know that he'd brought her to this low point. Maybe indirectly, but if he hadn't pushed her to come to the island, this might never have happened. He didn't know what to say to lighten her mood.

"Come on," he said finally, deciding that actions spoke louder than words. He climbed out of the Jeep and grabbed her suitcase. "Let me show you around."

Nick got Sal settled in the cabin, showing her the few amenities in a matter of a few minutes. He then excused himself to go outside and place a few phone calls while she unpacked and made herself comfortable in her temporary home.

By the time he returned to the cabin, he had lined up a few visitors for later. Much as he wanted to, he couldn't just leave her alone with whatever magic had sparked on arrival. Someone with more knowledge about such things than Nick had would have to evaluate her and any potential threat she might pose.

It wasn't long before their first guest arrived. Nick heard the Jeep coming and went out to meet it. One of his best men, a dark-haired jaguar named Mario, who was popular with the ladies, had volunteered to drive the visiting mage out to the cabin. Nick gave Mario the subtle hand signal that told him to wait while Nick escorted William Howell the Fourth, their new Alpha female's father and high-powered human mage, into the cabin.

"Sullivan Lane, this is Mr. Howell. He has probably forgotten more about magic than I will ever know. I'd like for you to talk with him, if you will," Nick asked politely, though all three of them knew she really had no choice.

Sal reached out a hand to make the mage's acquaintance and nearly jumped as sparks shot from her hand to the older man's. Sal looked horrified. Howell seemed intrigued.

"My, you do have some power, don't you?" Mr. Howell said almost absently as he regarded his fingers. "That stings," he went on, smiling at her. "How about you?"

Sal shook her hand a few times, her expression guarded. "Yeah, it tingles almost painfully," she agreed. "Sorry. I have no control over it, though this has never happened to me before. Not until I came here."

Howell shook his head, his expression friendly, but also curious. "I'm not surprised. This island is in a unique position. Lying smack dab along a ley line, if I'm not mistaken, and I believe the caldera of the volcano is a nexus point where earth magic spewed forth in ancient times to form this little bit of land. If I was a superstitious man, I might almost believe the island was created by Mother Earth with the jaguar people in mind. It's the perfect setting for them. Healing and protective. But, for humans like you and me, it has a tendency to wake things up that had been sleeping peacefully." He moved into the cabin and took the seat Nick gestured toward, still talking to Sal. "You've never used magic before, you say?"

Sal sat down opposite Howell, and Nick stood near the door, keeping one eye on Mario, who was scanning the perimeter, and one on the fascinating conversation happening inside. Nick had expected Mark to be their first visitor, but Howell was a smarter choice, by far. Nick just hadn't realized that Mark had grown to trust his new father-in-law so much while Nick was away in Hollywood. Apparently, he'd missed a great deal while he'd been on his mission for the Clan.

"I've been in denial, I guess," Sal stated, her tone making her sound very depressed. "My mother has had episodes of wild magic most of her life. When it happens, it makes her do bad things. Things that eventually led to her being locked up in a home for the criminally insane."

Howell shook his head, his expression speaking of sorrow and concern. "That's truly unfortunate. I suppose you believe all magic is evil as a result of your experiences?"

Sal nodded. "I don't want it. I've never wanted it. Not after what it did to my mother."

"First, my dear," Howell said in a fatherly way, sitting forward so he was a little bit closer to her. "Magic is neither good nor evil in its raw form. It's what we do with it. In your mother's case, I suspect she never received any training, and as a woman of great power… You know, the old saying is as true for us as it is for regular humans—with great power, comes great responsibility. In your mother's case, mages of high ability absolutely must be trained. If they are not, the magic they possess can be uncontrollable, and terrible things can happen, as I believe happened with your mother."

Nick was pleased to see that Sal was listening. For the first time since the sparks had appeared on the plane, someone was getting through to her.

"You really think so?" she asked, a small ray of hope sounding in her voice.

"I'd need to meet her and do some investigating of the circumstances surrounding her imprisonment, but my theory makes the most sense, barring any unknown information at this time. I can promise you, right now, that I will look into her circumstances. Perhaps there is something I can do to help her."

Sal's eyes widened, and that little ray of hope grew. "Thank you, Mr. Howell. I'm glad to pay for anything that might help her. I've been using my earnings to help make her life a little more comfortable, even in that place where they're keeping her. They allow me to supply soft clothing and bedding. It's not a prison, per se, but a private clinic with bars on the windows and multiple locks on the doors. The court ordered her to be held in a facility, but as I began to earn more money, I was able to improve the location and amenities. She also has to talk with doctors all the time, which I think is a good thing, since the consequences of the magical episodes have left her with nightmares and a lot of guilt. The therapy helps with that, at least."

Nick's heart softened when he heard the true love for her parent in Sal's voice. He hadn't realized where all her money was going. He'd been impressed that she hadn't blown her fortune on fast cars and ridiculous clothing, but he'd had no idea of the responsibility weighing her down. She'd spent her money making her mother more comfortable. If that wasn't a noble cause, Nick didn't know what was.

As the conversation turned more technical about magic

and the sensations Sal had been experiencing since arriving on the island, Nick took a moment to go outside and have a word with Mario. He wanted tighter patrols overnight. Nick, himself, would be staying in the cabin with Sal, but he was counting on his security people to patrol the perimeter, just in case Sal was able to sneak by him.

It shouldn't be possible, but then again, he had missed her innate magic. If he'd blundered that badly already, he wasn't going to take any chances that she could fool him again.

When Nick returned to the cabin just a few minutes later, he walked in on a surprising sight. Howell had somehow coaxed Sal into generating sparks again, this time held between her two hands. She was holding them, palms facing each other, and a glinting ball of energy was contained in the space between them.

Sweet Mother of All, she was already generating energy balls. He knew such things could be thrown with deadly accuracy by mages of evil intent. He shot Howell a questioning look, very concerned about this turn of events.

"It seems…" Howell said to him in a calm voice, his gaze staying on Sal even as he directed his words toward Nick. "Miss Lane is a natural."

Nick wasn't sure he liked the sound of that. A natural what? Destructive mage? Fireball thrower? Offensive power?

Howell didn't give him a chance to respond. He merely redirected his attention to Sal. "Good," he told her. "Now, let it dissipate. The way I showed you."

Before Nick's eyes, the energy began to fade. He'd never seen anything like it, and the burgeoning control she must have achieved in order to do it impressed him. She could douse the sparks now, without releasing them to potentially do harm. That was a hell of an improvement for just a few minutes of instruction.

"You sure you never did this before?" Nick asked her, unable to keep the suspicion out of his tone.

Sal looked hurt when she met his gaze. "Of course not. I've done all I could to keep magic as far away from me as possible, all my life. This is totally new to me, and definitely not welcome." She sighed, softening her tone. "But, if I have to deal with this, I will. Mr. Howell has been kind enough to teach me a few things, which have already made a positive impact. I just might survive this, if I can manage to control it."

"Of course you will, my dear," Howell said in a joyful tone. "Magic has been used by mortals for centuries. You will learn to control it and be able to have a normal life. What happened to your mother is a tragedy, but it's important you realize that it was preventable, if only she'd had the proper instruction."

"Could she learn now?" Sal asked, the ball of energy completely gone as she lowered her hands.

"Possibly," Howell answered. "But, to know for certain, I would have to meet her. Perhaps that is something we could arrange for later, after your visit to the island is complete. I haven't been out to Hollywood in many years. I think I would enjoy a little trip. Especially if it meant we could help an unfortunate victim of her own power." He shook his head again, a sad expression on his face.

Howell stood and dusted imaginary lint off his sleeve. "Well, that's enough for now. I want you to practice what I've shown you, and if you have the least discomfort, I want you to call me, no matter what time it is. I'm just a short Jeep ride away, staying up at the mansion to visit with my daughter and new son-in-law. She's learning about magic, too, so perhaps you'll have something in common when you get a chance to meet."

Nick frowned. Right now, he wasn't sure if Sal would ever be cleared to meet their new Alpha female, Mark's mate, Shelly. But he didn't say anything. He had to see how things went with Sal first. Only after a bit more observation would he make the determination as to whether or not she could be trusted around the heart of the Clan.

Howell left a few minutes later, after shaking hands—no sparks this time—with Sal and Nick in farewell. Mario left, driving Howell away but nodding to Nick in a way that let him know his orders had been passed along and were in the process of being implemented.

"This is fun, but I really need to stretch my legs," Sal said when he turned back toward the main part of the cabin.

The original structure had increased in size with the addition of two small bedrooms and a full bath attached by doorways to the main room. The cabin had been decorated with modern furnishings, and one wall had been turned into a small kitchenette, complete with electric stove, pantry storage and a mini refrigerator. It was a comfortable place, but after the long flight, Nick could definitely understand the desire to walk around outside for a bit.

"If you don't mind company, I'll go with you. It's pretty easy to get turned around in the jungle, and we deliberately keep it kind of wild out there. You might also stumble across some of my Clan brothers and sisters in their fur, and I wouldn't want them to startle you." Nick hoped for her agreement. He would hate to have to insist, but he would do so, if necessary.

"Sure. I could use a guide," she answered casually.

She stood, reaching above her head, stretching the long, luscious lines of her body. Nick had to look away as his libido kicked into high gear.

He kept himself on a short leash while they walked around the perimeter of the cabin. He pointed out some of the local flowers and plants. He also noticed some of his security team stalking through the jungle in their cat forms, but Sal seemed not to see them. Nick hadn't really expected her to be able to pick out a jaguar in the jungle, but he watched her closely, just in case.

By the time they got back from their gentle stroll through the countryside, another vehicle was pulling up in front of the cabin. If his nose didn't deceive him, Nick surmised someone in the kitchens back at the mansion had taken pity on them and sent provisions.

Sure enough, it was young Janice at the wheel of the all-terrain vehicle. Her mother, Marie, was the chef who always cooked for the Alpha. Mark took Marie with him wherever he went around the world. She was his personal chef, and one of the many lines of defense that kept the billionaire businessman and Alpha of the jaguar Clan safe.

Nick went to meet Janice and help her unload the huge basket of food that had been strapped to the back of her four-wheeler. Janice didn't linger, though he could tell she was curious about Sal. Still, word must have reached her that their newest guest was off limits for the moment. Janice simply handed off the supplies and got back on her all-terrain vehicle, turning it around in a tight circle before heading back the way she had come.

Nick carried the big basket into the cabin. Sal had already gone in, probably realizing that Nick wasn't going to be making introductions this time. He tried to ignore the hurt look on her face. It couldn't be helped. He still didn't have enough data to make a sound judgment on whether or not Sal posed a danger to the Clan.

Sighing, he set about putting away the groceries. The little refrigerator had reached temperature and was more than ready for the covered dishes and perishables that had been included in the care package. Nick also found two of Marie's famous gourmet sandwiches, along with a few readymade side dishes. He set those on the table in the small kitchen area. It was close enough to dinnertime that they would both probably enjoy a meal.

The Texas takeout had been hours ago, and as the sun started to set, they sat down to share the catered meal at the small table.

CHAPTER 12

Night fell quickly. They had spent most of the day traveling, and it had been chaos since they'd arrived on the island. At least, her mind had been in chaos. Magic. Mages. Magic lessons.

It was like something out of one of her nightmares. Nick seemed to be taking it all in stride, but he was definitely mad at her. He did his best to be civil, but she could tell he was pissed.

At her? At the situation? At magic in general? She didn't really know, but how she wished she could go back in time to this morning, when it really looked like they we're working toward something special. Together.

She had gotten her hopes up. She'd been fantasizing about Nick from almost the first moment she'd seen him. He was a powerful figure. A devastating man in so many ways. Attractive didn't even begin to cover it.

And, when she'd learned about him being a shapeshifter... Somehow, that didn't seem like the more familiar, much scarier magic she'd seen in her life. If he was magical, it wasn't in the same way as her mother. He was in control.

It was that control over himself and his surroundings that had drawn her in. Sal liked thinking she was in charge of her own life. She realized now that she'd been fooling herself all

124

along. Managing her environment and her path in life had been a driving force in her existence from the first time her mother's wild magic had gotten them both in trouble.

She'd only been a little girl then, but when her mother's magic lashed out and destroyed a display of glassware in a store they had been shopping in, Sal had taken the blame, sensing that something wasn't quite right with her mother. Mama had paid for the broken items, even though they didn't have much money to spare, and they'd been allowed to go on their way.

But life had changed at that moment. Oh, it had taken a while before the truly horrific magic had manifested, but Sal had always thought about the glass incident as the turning point. That had been the first time the magic had reached out and done damage. It had been a downhill slide since then as her mother's ability to hold the destruction at bay had deteriorated over time, culminating in tragedy.

These deep thoughts were running through her brain as they ate dinner in near total silence. It had been a long day, and she was both mentally and physically exhausted. Too much had happened in the short time since she'd left California. She'd had her own turning point with magic today, and the fear that the rest of her days would be a mirror of the downhill path her mother's life had taken sat heavily on her mind. She'd always carried that fear with her, but today she'd learned there might be another outcome. An outcome where she could control the wild magic, not be controlled by it.

She was in no mood to talk about it, though. Not with Nick. Not with anybody.

But, as they finished eating, there was a knock at the door of the cabin. *What now?*

Sal wasn't sure she could take much more. She looked at Nick, but his expression told her nothing as he stood from the table and went to answer the door.

Her back was to the door, and she didn't have the energy or desire to turn around and spy on them like a busybody. If whoever it was had come to see her, she'd find out soon enough. The low murmur of male voices was in the background as she finished the last few bites of her sandwich, after which she sat back in her chair, waiting to find out what would happen next.

What she really wanted was a long, hot bath, followed by a comfy bed and the blissful oblivion of sleep. Somehow, she didn't think she was going to get that anytime soon.

"How is she?" Mark asked without preliminaries when Nick opened the door.

He'd sensed his friend and Alpha approaching through the forest. He must've driven partway up the trail then come in on foot—probably to check in with the jaguars stationed around the perimeter. Mark was good at details like that. It was part of what made him a great Alpha. He was more hands-on with his people than any humans observing the billionaire businessman would have thought.

"At this point, I think she's exhausted. It was a long trip, and then, all hell broke loose when we got here." Nick ran one hand through his short hair in fatigued frustration. "Sending Howell over was a masterstroke, though. The magic practice seemed to settle her a bit. I get the feeling Miss Lane is someone who likes to be in control of herself at all times, and when the sparks started flying, she sort of freaked out."

Mark frowned. "The island affected my mate in a similar way, but she didn't have any knowledge of magic. Her father had been protecting her all her life, and although it was startling, I don't think she had any fear. From what Howell said when he got back to the mansion, Miss Lane has a very real aversion—even a hatred—of magic. She knows about it and has only ever seen the bad side." Mark looked past Nick into the room, his gaze settling on Sal's back with the merest hint of compassion. "Hastings is running a more detailed background check on her. Once he knew where to look, it was a lot simpler to discover the holes in the story she had fabricated. He's compiling a report that he'll send through shortly, but the bare bones of what she told you about her mother are already confirmed. Hastings has located the mom and is working on getting copies of her medical and police reports. There's also a money trail, leading from Miss Lane to the care facilities her mother's been in over the years."

Nick nodded. This was good news, if there was anything good about finding out she'd been lying to him. Even if it was only a lie of omission. She really had been just protecting her mother's secret. And she hadn't just been lying to him. She'd been telling the same story to everyone.

She'd buried her dark secret so well, and so far down, that nobody had been able to discover it yet. Perhaps, they never would. For her sake, Nick hoped the press never got a hold of her tragic past. Sal would never be able to put it behind her if that happened.

He knew all about protecting a celebrity. The bad stuff from the past never quite stayed buried. Whenever a new story came out, there were always references to things that had happened many years ago.

In Mark's case, they'd been extremely careful to create a public persona that could withstand any investigation done by human means. Nick wasn't as sure about the methods Sal had used to hide her own background. Once this situation was settled—if she was still talking to him—Nick would do his best to make sure both Sal and her mother were protected.

Though confused by the fact that she'd been lying to him, his inner cat still insisted that she was his mate. Perhaps more now than ever. After the magic had manifested, the jaguar had become even more interested—if that was possible—in her as a life partner.

His human side was a lot more reticent. Oh, he was still attracted to her. He'd have to be dead or blind or both not to notice how alluring she was. She also stimulated his mind, and he had enjoyed talking with her on so many occasions. She had a quick wit that he admired and didn't take herself, or her newfound celebrity, too seriously. That was incredibly appealing.

"You sure you want to talk to her?" Nick asked Mark,

both of them keeping their voices low enough that she would not be able to hear what they were saying.

"Might as well." Mark shrugged. "I'd like to form my own opinion about her."

"I expected nothing less," Nick agreed, opening the door wider. There wasn't much left to say that couldn't be said in front of her.

Mark walked into the cabin. At the same time, Sal stood from her chair and turned toward the doorway.

"Mark, this is Sullivan Lane. Sal, this is Mark." Nick made the casual introductions. He noticed that Mark didn't move closer to her or offer his hand. She stood her ground, as well.

"I'm pleased to meet you, Mr. Pepard. Thank you for your hospitality. I'm sorry my arrival has created difficulties for us both." Her tone was steady, but Nick heard the bitterness just under the surface.

"Good to meet you, too, Miss Lane. My wife is a big fan," Mark told her. Nick's eyebrow rose in surprise. He hadn't known Shelly was a fan of Sal's movies.

After the pleasantries were out of the way, Mark asked some very direct questions designed to elicit honest responses. From what Nick now knew about Sal, she gave Mark truthful answers. She probably realized by this time that lying to them would cause nothing but more trouble.

Sal looked even more weary by the time Mark finished with her. The Alpha seemed satisfied, though, which set Nick's inner jaguar more at ease. The cat understood—better than the human side—that the Alpha's instincts were even better than his own.

Mark left them not long after he'd arrived. His questioning hadn't lasted too long, and when he turned to go, Sal looked bemused more than annoyed. Nick closed the door after Mark and turned back to find Sal cleaning up the dishes they had used. She hummed softly to herself as she tidied up the kitchen area. Nick was loath to interrupt. She seemed at peace for the first time since arriving on the island. He didn't want to ruin the few minutes of comfort she'd had all evening.

Eventually, though, everything had been put away. There hadn't been that much to clean, after all. Sal turned toward him and leaned one hip against the kitchen counter.

"I'm tired," she said. "If there's nothing else, I'd like to get some sleep."

"By all means," Nick said, gesturing toward the bedroom doorways on the other side of the cabin. "Don't let me stop you. I've got some work to do before I turn in, but make yourself comfortable. I'll keep the noise level down and try not to disturb you."

Sal left without further comment, heading for the bedroom she had chosen earlier. Nick watched her go with regret in his heart. He'd had such high hopes when they left California. Now, it looked like his desire for her would have to wait until things were more settled. The question of her magic stood between them. An emphatic obstacle that could bar his path to future mated bliss.

If he let it. Or if fate was unkind.

Nick set up his laptop and began scrolling through email. Hastings had sent several updates throughout the evening. Nick opened them one at a time and read each word with great interest. Slowly, the pieces of Sal's past were falling into place. Hastings commented several times on how impressed he was with the way Sal had hidden her tracks.

That made Nick feel marginally better about having missed the signs, but he was still kicking himself for not looking closer into her background. He'd dropped the ball in a big way, and he was just lucky that, so far, it hadn't come back to kick him in the ass.

A while later, his cell phone rang. He hushed the ringer and answered the call when he saw it was Mark.

"My father-in-law just got off a conference call with a trusted associate of his in the magical community out on the West Coast. Seems they were aware of a rogue mage getting into trouble with the law about a decade ago, but it was decided the case was too high profile to intervene. Apparently, they have some sort of council out there that watches over mages in the area. They didn't know about Miss Lane's mother until all hell started breaking loose, and by then, the human authorities were heavily involved. They've been monitoring her for years now, ever since she was committed. It's unclear whether they planned to do anything about her situation, but they were aware of it and made all the proper noises of sympathy to Howell on the phone just now." The disgust came through easily in Mark's voice.

"Mages aren't like us, Mark," Nick reminded his best friend and leader. "There's no sense of Clan. No feeling of family unless they truly are blood related. From what Sal told me and what Hastings has confirmed already, it was just Sal and her mom. The dad was long gone, and the mom's family was all dead. Without blood relations, they were all alone in the world. It's just a shame someone didn't step forward to help them when they needed it most."

"Amen to that," Mark agreed. "Humans can be very cruel. I mean, it's pretty clear they saw her struggling, and those other mages might have been able to help her, but nobody had the balls to step forward."

"What does Howell say about it?" Nick wondered.

"He's mad. He's said some very uncomplimentary things about the mage council out there. I get the feeling what little respect he might've had for them has now disappeared. He also seems to be very sympathetic to Sal's problem and her mother's fate. I think he's planning some sort of rescue." Mark chuckled. "Don't worry. I won't let him attempt it alone. If Miss Lane's mother can be rehabilitated, we'll do all we can to help. She may not be a jaguar, but nobody deserves to be locked up for something they don't know how to control, if there's another possibility."

"Thanks, Mark," Nick said quietly.

"Why is this so important to you, Nick?" Mark asked, his tone both resigned and curious.

Nick sighed before replying, taking his time to gather his thoughts and find the right words. This was going to be hard. Nick had to admit why he had screwed up so badly and take ownership of his mistakes.

"My instincts are screaming that she's my mate, Mark. But the situation is so fucked up right now," he admitted, self-recrimination in his voice. "I think I've been blinded to all these problems because of my attraction to her, and I know that's not good enough. Not for the Clan. Not for you, Mark. If you want me to step down and put someone else in as your head of security, I'll understand. I've failed you and the Clan on this mission, and I couldn't be sorrier if I tried."

Mark was silent a long moment, but his next words surprised Nick.

"You found your mate?" Mark's tone was filled with the mix of satisfaction and joy. How could the Alpha be happy for him when Nick had failed so miserably?

"Yeah, I think so," Nick replied, ignoring the rest for the moment. "If she'll even speak to me after all this."

"If she's truly your mate, she will. I have no doubt," Mark told him. "I didn't think a human—even one with mage power—could feel the same depth of emotion, the same profound bond as we shifters, but I was wrong. I've felt it now, and I sincerely hope that you discover the truth of my words as soon as possible. Your life is about to change, my friend, for the better."

"Maybe." Nick wasn't willing to believe just yet. There were too many hurdles to cross first.

"As for replacing you with someone else... That ain't gonna happen. There's nobody I trust more to watch my back and see to the Clan's safety than you, Nick."

"Even after I screwed up so bad?" Nick was surprised by Mark's lenient attitude. The Alpha wasn't known for cutting anybody who had messed up any slack.

"She's your mate, Nick. Allowances have to be made in a case like this. Plus, being that she is your mate, she couldn't possibly be doing anything to actively hurt the Clan. It's just not possible, and I won't believe it. Not after mating myself. Take it from the wise old married man. The Goddess doesn't bring people together arbitrarily. Matings are made in heaven and designed with a purpose. I firmly believe that."

Mark was talking nonsense. He'd gone all mystical like this a few times since his mating, but Nick had always been able to ignore it before now. Then again… Maybe Mark did know more about how mating worked than Nick did. The Alpha often knew more about arcane subject matter than the mere head of his security detail.

"All right," Nick allowed. "I'm not saying I believe everything you've been spewing, but I'm willing to give it the benefit of the doubt. And thanks for not firing me. I'll do better from now on. Promise."

"I know," Mark replied, a certain smugness in his tone that Nick studiously ignored. "As for your lady, Howell was favorably impressed by her. He said she was the fastest study he'd ever seen, but he was certain she had known nothing about magic—except maybe the bad stuff she'd seen happen with her mother—before he started teaching her the basics. He's already volunteered to give her more training, if she's agreeable."

"Do you think it's wise to give her more control over something potentially destructive?" Nick asked, doing his job to protect the Clan, even though it meant possibly hurting Sal. The conflict made his inner cat want to yowl, but he ignored it, waiting for the answer to his question.

"We really have no choice. We can't let her go back to her life as if nothing's happened. Howell tells me that, now that her magic has been awakened, it won't be easy to subdue it again. That cat's well and truly out of the bag." Regret sounded in Mark's voice. "However, I think it would be beneficial to all of us to let her learn some control. Howell is a top-level mage. He's been showing Shelly all sorts of cool stuff about her heritage and her powers. I think he can be trusted to give your Sal the tools she needs to control the monster that might've just been unleashed. We don't want what happened to her mother happening to her, too."

"Yeah." Nick shook his head. That would be a terrible outcome to this difficult situation.

"I won't invite her up to the mansion just yet. I'm still a bit too protective of my new mate, and my jaguar would go nuts at the possible threat. But I'm willing—and more importantly, Howell is willing—to let her learn from him up there at the cabin. He's agreed to trek over there each day to give her lessons, if she wants to learn more."

"That's great," Nick said quietly. "I'll ask her, but I believe she'll say yes. She's very afraid that the magic will ruin her life the way it ruined her mother's. She looked a lot better after the little bit Howell taught her today. I think she'll want to learn more."

At that point, Nick became aware of Sal. She had come into the main part of the cabin from the bedroom she'd chosen. Scented, steamy air wafted from the bathroom, too, as if she'd taken a bath with some sort of scented oil.

His imagination kicked into overdrive just thinking about it. Warm, sudsy water. Slick, soft skin. Nick had to clear his throat before he could speak again.

He was probably taking the coward's way out, but Nick ended the phone call quickly. Mark would understand. He had a mate of his own. Besides, they'd said all that needed saying tonight. They wouldn't be able to make any more decisions until they had more data, and that would have to wait until tomorrow.

Nick laid his phone down on the table. He was done for the night, unless something urgent came up. As a shifter, he handled fatigue better than most humans, but he'd also been on the road—or, at least, in the sky—most of the day. It was time to rest.

Or maybe it was time to see just where he stood with Sal.

CHAPTER 13

Sal wasn't sure why she'd gone back into the main area of the cabin after her bath, but there she was, staring at the back of Nick's head as he sat at the table. He tensed, so she figured he must've heard her come into the room.

She'd wanted to go to sleep. She was weary enough. But something was bothering her. It was calling her. Making her want to spend more time with Nick, even if he didn't like her that much right now. She was still drawn to him. Impossible as it was.

"You're right," she said without preamble. "What Mr. Howell showed me was important. I feel it in my bones, and I *do* want to know more." She walked farther into the room. Nick's head turned to follow her progress as she walked around the table to face him.

"Would you say your instincts are pointing you toward learning more about magic?" he asked, a crafty look in his eye that she didn't quite understand.

"My instincts say it's important to learn from *him*. Mr. Howell is one of the good guys," she allowed, sitting down opposite him.

Nick grinned faintly. "I told you. We allow only white-hatted cowboys on this island."

"Then, why did you let me come? When you didn't know,

and probably still can't say for sure, if I'm good or bad?"

"You've got your instincts, and I've got mine," he told her. "My instincts say you're on the right side, even if there's evidence to the contrary." He grimaced. "You've got me in knots, Sal. My cat side can't believe anything bad of you, yet my human side knows you were keeping things from me and isn't sure exactly why. Was it merely to protect your mother and your secret? Or was there something more sinister behind your lies?"

Now, that hurt. Sal got up from the table, humiliated. "For the record, I never lied to you. I just didn't tell you everything. There's a difference. And, though I doubt you'll take my word for anything at this point, my only motivation, all this time, has been protecting my mom. *Merely* doesn't even come close to describing the importance I place on her. She's my *mother*."

Sal would have stormed out gracefully, but somehow, Nick was out of his chair and standing directly in front of her, blocking her path. He moved like the cat that shared his soul. Fast and soundless, even in human form. It was more than a little scary. Sal caught her breath in surprise.

"There's also this…"

He lifted one hand toward her, gently stroking her cheek with the backs of his fingers. The touch was gossamer light, tender in a way no man had ever been with her, and utterly enchanting. The look in his gaze as it met and held hers was molten. Intense, swirling magic shone from within, letting her know the cat was there, present in the man. She was speechless—anything she might've said caught in a suddenly dry throat.

"You confuse me on every level, Sal," he whispered. "I want you. Have wanted you since the moment we met and I first caught your unique scent. That's how we know when someone is special. Our cats recognize something in their scent. I can't explain it any better than that, but it's part of our unique magic."

She didn't like the sound of that. Years of cringing away

from anything even remotely related to magic had preconditioned her response. He must have seen something in her eyes because he soothed her, placing both hands on her shoulders and rubbing in small, comforting circles.

"Come on, now," he coaxed. "After everything you've learned about the world—my world—in the past day, you have to realize that not all magic is bad. Shifters have a unique sort of power. It's part of us. It's what allows us to change form at will, but for the vast majority of us, it's not something we consciously control, like mages do. We're not spell-casters or potion-makers. We don't put hexes on people. And we definitely don't use magic—or let it use us—in the way it's affected your family. It's just something that's part of us. That makes us who we are."

She swallowed hard. "I see that intellectually, but it's hard to put aside the beliefs of a lifetime," she told him.

"I won't hurt you, Sal. Not ever," he told her. "Although, I might have to keep you away from my Clan." He looked a bit sheepish as he glanced around the cabin. "But I want you to know... If we can't resolve this situation, and you have to leave the island, I'll go with you. I'd give up my Clan in a heartbeat, if you asked me to."

Sal's breath caught. What was he saying? Was he truly willing to give up his family, his people, his duty...for her?

Sweet heaven! Was he feeling this, too? The almost uncontrollable attraction that made her want to drop everything and just run into his arms. Damn the consequences. Damn everything except the two of them...together...for all time.

A fairytale. That's what it was. She had to be delusional to think he was feeling the same ridiculous urges she was. It just made no sense.

Nick drew closer...and closer. And then, his lips touched hers.

Fireworks. And tingles. Little zaps of magic sparkled where his lips tentatively met hers. He went slow, as if waiting for permission before he proceeded. Not wanting to wait, she threw her arms around his shoulders and drew him closer. She couldn't make it any plainer than that, and he seemed to read her message loud and clear as he tugged her even closer and melded their lips more firmly together.

Then, their mouths opened as if in perfect accord. The magic flared, but she knew how to control it now. Even that short practice with Mr. Howell had awoken her instincts, and the older mage had convinced her to trust them. So, when the magic rose, she let instinct lead the way, and it went from potentially problematic to harmless little energizing zaps kept between them.

She pressed as close to him as she possibly could, wanting to climb all over him, but there was too much fabric between their bodies. He deepened the kiss, and her head spun as he picked her up. She had no real sense of where he was taking her, but she hoped it was to one of the side rooms. Preferably one with a bed in it, and soft sheets.

When he lay her down on a bed a few moments later, it was as if her wish had been granted by a hunky genie. The sheets were as luxurious as she could've hoped for, but she had no idea about the rest of the room. Frankly, she didn't care. As long as they could share this king-sized bed and get naked together, all would be right with her world.

Nick continued to kiss her as he took her down to the mattress, his hands powerful yet gentle as he guided them both to the downy surface. She pushed at his clothing, wanting it gone, but he wasn't cooperating. This called for more drastic measures.

Unbuckling his belt, she slid her hand downward, into his pants, and wrapped around the hard length she found straining toward her. He groaned. Or maybe it was a growl. She couldn't be absolutely sure, but the sound made her nipples peak and her insides squirm with heat.

Nick was sexier than she'd imagined—and she'd *imagined* quite a bit. She'd been having fantasies about the man almost non-stop from the night they'd shared that fateful cup of tea.

He'd intrigued her, made her flush with the thoughts

running through her mind when she watched him move, the powerful lean muscles moving under the fabric of his clothing. Nick was *hot* with a capital H, and she'd noticed. Oh, boy, had she noticed!

She squeezed his length, hoping to get his attention. With any luck, he'd figure out that, while she was really enjoying his kisses and the way his body loomed over her, making her feel delicate and protected, what she really wanted was access to more skin. For both of them.

"Are you rushing me, doll?" Nick whispered against her lips. She could feel the curve of his smile against her mouth.

"Want to touch you." She gasped as one of his hands moved downward to cup the area between her thighs, right through the fabric of her pants.

"I believe you *are* touching me, sweetness." His voice sounded almost like it was underpinned by a feline purr. Was that even possible?

"Not enough. Want more."

She could barely string together complete sentences. He'd reduced her to a simpleton, and she hadn't even taken her clothes off yet. Would she even survive this? She had no idea, but she definitely needed to find out.

She squirmed against him, and he chuckled. "All right, princess. I'll give you what you want. What we *both* want." He nibbled on her lips then moved away. "I'd just thought I'd try to go slow this first time, for your sake. You are only human, after all," he said, the teasing look in his eyes daring her to object.

"Come back here and see what this mere human can do, big boy."

Now, where had *that* come from?

That line was like something out of a movie script, but she couldn't remember ever saying anything even remotely like that to any of the few lovers she'd had over the years. She might act bold in her movies, but Sal was a bit...um...conservative when it came to the men she'd slept with and how she'd acted around them.

Seemed like Nick brought out all sorts of new facets she hadn't known existed in her. First, the lust, when she'd been watching him the past couple of weeks. Then, the magic, when they arrived on this crazy island. And now, the femme fatale with the quick quips. She hadn't known she had it in her.

Nick eased her hand out of his pants then stood, rising gracefully to his feet at the side of the bed. When his fingers went to the buttons on his shirt and began to slowly undo them one by one, her mouth went dry. His molten gaze held hers as he pulled the tails of the shirt out of his pants and opened it completely.

His chest was a work of art. His abs were the kind that Hollywood hunks spend hours in the gym trying to get—and failing. When he shrugged the shirt off his shoulders, the saliva returned to her mouth in a wave. He definitely had drool-worthy shoulders and biceps. She just wanted to lick him all over and find out if his muscles were as hard as they looked.

She'd never seen such a specimen of a man—including the overly-ripped actors she'd worked with. They were skinny string beans compared to Nick. All man. All muscle. Lean, mean, fighting machine.

And he was all hers. At least for tonight. Sal promised herself she'd make the most of this once-in-a-lifetime opportunity while she could.

She had no illusions that the passions of the moment would lift when the sun rose. He might be willing to say he'd give up everything for her if he had to in the heat of the moment tonight, but tomorrow, when they'd sated their lust for each other and real life returned with a bang, things would likely be very different.

She didn't blame him for that. That's just the way it would probably go down, and she had to prepare herself to be fine with it. No matter how much it might hurt.

But for right now, she would enjoy the man candy in front of her eyes. He smiled a lazy, secretive smile as he threw the shirt behind him then started slowly on the zipper of his pants. She'd already unbuckled his belt and undid the clasp at the top, but she hadn't had the patience to deal with the zipper.

Nick took it down, one tooth at a time, the little snicks of sound overly loud in the quiet of the night. She found herself holding her breath as he lowered that zipper, hanging on every motion as if her life depended on it. What would be revealed when it came all the way down?

She'd felt what had to be the biggest, hardest cock she'd ever had the good fortune to handle. Would he look as good as he'd felt? She'd bet good money that answer was an emphatic *yes*. Everything about Nick was almost too good to be true. Why should this be any different?

The white of his underwear blocked her view as the last tooth of the zipper snicked free. But not for long. Nick hooked his thumbs beneath the waistbands of the tighty whities and the pants and shoved them both down together, stepping his long legs out of the fabric and leaving it on the floor.

When he straightened, he seemed to pause, letting her get a good long look at him. It was immediately clear that, with a body like that, Nick had absolutely nothing to hide. He was magnificent.

Every muscle was in perfect proportion. His great height was balanced by his lithe musculature. He was Adonis. Michelangelo's David. The epitome of male perfection.

And he was coming for her. She couldn't wait.

Nick stalked forward like the jaguar that lived in his soul. Soundless. Intent. Sure of himself and his acceptance.

And why wouldn't he be? She'd given him every indication of her desire. She wanted him, and she didn't want to wait.

Nick reached her, continuing his stalk right up onto the bed, where he crouched over her. She felt trapped, but not in a bad way. She knew he'd move aside the moment she became uncomfortable, but she wasn't in the least wary of him right now. No, she was totally on board with the way he covered her, leaving room for her to look and feel—and room for him to do away with her clothing.

Praise the lord! She was finally going to get skin to skin with him.

She tried to help, but her fingers fumbled, excitement slowing her down and making her clumsy. Nick took care of her, removing her outer garments with the utmost care. Her breath caught multiple times as he turned the simple act of undressing into a sensual delight that couldn't compare with anything she had ever experienced before.

No other lover had been this attentive, this tender, this...perfect. Only Nick. And they hadn't even really gotten started yet. Sal mentally strapped herself in and prepared for a wild ride.

She almost couldn't believe they were actually doing this. She'd dreamed about it many times but had never really expected it to happen. Fantasies were one thing. Reality, in her experience, was quite another. Reality had always been disappointing, but she had a feeling her luck was about to change. In a big way.

Nick lowered the straps of her bra one at a time, as if he was savoring the moment and giving her plenty of time to feel every little motion and anticipate what would come next. By the time he bared her breasts, she was a quivering, super-sensitive bundle of nerves just waiting to be soothed by his breath, his touch...his tongue.

He kissed every inch of skin he exposed, laving her nipples as if they had all night for him to do just that. But she wanted more. So much more.

She made impatient sounds in the back of her throat, and he answered her with a deep rumbling purr that vibrated through his chest, making her shiver. His inner cat was definitely enjoying this, which made her feel better about not reciprocating right away. It was all she could do to lay back and enjoy what he was doing to her. She felt so boneless, she could barely lift a finger at the moment. While she wanted to touch him the way he was touching her, it would have to wait until she had better control over her limbs.

Fortunately, he didn't seem to mind at all. In fact, it felt like his main goal was to pleasure her right now. The rest would come later.

An unselfish lover was something new in her experience. She'd known Nick was special, but this just drove home to her how very different he was from other men.

Then, he removed her pants and panties in one long pull, and she was totally bare before him. He hadn't taken his time with her pants like he'd done with her top. No, he was starting to look like a hungry predator, too long denied. And she was feeling about the same, if not worse. He'd driven her too high already. She needed completion. She needed relief from the tension he had built so expertly. And she needed it now.

Reaching forward, Sal grabbed him by the shoulders, dragging him down over her. She sought his lips in a hard kiss that spoke of her urgency and need. Thankfully, he seemed to understand. Either that or he felt exactly the same way, because a moment later, that magnificently hard cock she'd had in her hand earlier was probing the entrance of her willing body.

He joined them together, going slowly, but with steady pressure, until they were one. Then, he paused, looking downward to meet her gaze. A timeless moment stretched between them.

Peripherally, she was aware of sparkling light surrounding them, touching her skin, making it tingle. Magic, she realized. Coming from her. Created by her reaction to this incredible man and his tender loving.

Benevolent magic, touching, sensitizing, even encouraging. It was a wonder to her that such a thing could exist, when she'd always associated magic with terrible things.

One part of her mind was able to identify the source of the light and the champagne-like bubbles tingling against her skin, but the rest was firmly focused on Nick. He began to move, his sinuous muscles taking her in a way she had never before experienced. Everything with Nick was a new adventure, a new horizon. He made it special and unique.

After all the buildup, she came to a quick peak, but it wasn't over. Not by a long shot. Nick continued to thrust, varying his speed and angle, testing different motions to see what she liked best and what brought them both the most sensation. He was learning her, teaching her and pleasuring her all at the same time.

He was magnificent. And with him, she discovered things she had never known about her body, and his, and the capacity for bliss they shared together. She stroked him, petting his hard muscles and smooth skin, enjoying the way his purring increased as he drove them both higher.

She climaxed again and again as he continued the steady push toward some goal only he could see. She was eager to learn where he would take her, and her body responded to every challenge his posed, showing her that what she'd taken for fulfillment in the past was only a paltry example of something she'd never fully understood.

It was Nick. Only Nick, who could drive her to these heights and catch her while she fell. She screamed his name as she came for the final and most devastating time. She thought she heard him call out for her, as well, but she was close to mindless at that moment and couldn't be certain.

White light engulfed them. A benevolent shower of sparks filled the small room, bathing them in glory, warming them with an amazing peaceful magic that she had never known existed.

As she came apart in Nick's arms and he caught her, all was right with her world. Finally. Forever.

Nick had never purred in human form before, and that's when he knew what his instincts had been telling him for a while now was absolutely true. Sal was his mate. The one. The only. Forevermore.

Now, he just had to find a way to make it happen—and still retain his Clan, if at all possible. Of course, if it couldn't work out, he'd give up his friends and family for her. That hadn't been an impulsive claim. It was the absolute truth. Clan was one thing—and it would be very hard to say goodbye—but mating...mating was something special that only came along once in a lifetime if a shifter was very, very lucky.

Mates came above all else. They were sacred. Goddess-blessed. The others would understand if he chose her over the Clan. They'd accept, even if they wished it could be otherwise.

But it would all depend on her and what happened with her magic. It would also depend on whether or not she felt and recognized the bond that had been forged between them just now. He felt the connection like a pulsing heartbeat shared between them.

Nick worried that it might just be a shifter thing, though Mark had claimed his human mate said she felt it, too. Would Sal? His entire future was riding on it.

"Will you stay with me, in my bed, tonight?" he asked her after they had both calmed down a bit and were laying together, cuddling a bit. He felt nervous as a teenager with his first girl.

"Just try and kick me out," she responded, a challenging note of humor in her voice as she snuggled closer.

She sounded sleepy and sated, and his inner caveman wanted to pound on his chest with glee. He'd done that. He'd satisfied his mate so completely she was even now falling asleep in his arms. He watched her for long moments, basking in the glow for a while, until he joined her in sleep.

He woke her a couple more times in the night for more leisurely loving. She rose to meet him every time and began to push him for more. She touched him in ways he'd dreamed about since meeting her. She drove him wild with her gentle touch. So few people in his life had ever touched him with tenderness. It was significant to him that Sal did so.

Perhaps she was feeling something for him? He would do all in his power to make that happen because, more than anything, he wanted her to feel the mate bond and agree to be his forever.

Finally, they slept, twined together as close as he'd ever been with anyone, until well after dawn.

It was a knock on the door of the cabin that finally awakened Nick, sometime around nine a.m. He left the bed as quietly as possible, figuring to let Sal sleep more, if she could, while he went to see who was at the door.

If whoever it was had gotten close enough to knock, Nick must've really been sleeping hard. Normally, he'd awaken at the slightest sound his sensitive shifter hearing could pick up. That meant the crunch of feet walking toward the cabin should have been enough to wake him. The fact that it hadn't meant he'd let his guard down completely.

On the one hand, he was fascinated by the idea that being with Sal had allowed him to relax so completely. On the other, it was damned dangerous and not a good precedent to set. He had a job to do, and a mate to protect. He couldn't allow himself to slip so badly like this.

He'd been messing up a lot since Sal had come into his life. He supposed he should cut himself a little slack, considering finding one's mate was bound to mess with your head. Still, Nick couldn't afford to be sloppy. Not like this. Not with her safety, and the security of the entire Clan, on his shoulders.

Then again, they were on Jaguar Island. If he had to have a lapse in his usual vigilance, this was the place to do it. Nobody could get to her here. She was as safe as he could make her. Maybe that's why his subconscious mind had allowed his guard to fall so completely.

Nick wrapped a fallen sheet around his hips as he went to answer the door. Nakedness wasn't normally a problem among shifters, but it just might be Shelly's dad at the door. No way would Nick want to flash Mr. Howell and make the old man uncomfortable. Not when he was helping Sal so much.

But when he opened the door, it was Mario on the other

side, grinning like a fool. He gave Nick—and his sadly lacking attire—the full once over before lifting a picnic basket in one hand.

"I come bearing breakfast," he said, still smiling to beat the band as he pushed past Nick into the cabin. He headed for the kitchenette to put down the basket then turned to Nick. "Sorry if I interrupted...uh...anything. Did you have a good night with the movie star?"

"None of your damned business," Nick growled.

He didn't really mind the teasing. Mario was a good guy, and Nick was sure the rest of his security team was going to be razzing him about this, too, but he didn't want Sal to hear. Who knew how she might react? Right now, he didn't want to upset her. The relationship was too new to rock the boat just yet.

"Why don't you get me up to speed?" Nick redirected his subordinate. "Anything happen overnight that I should know about?"

"Nothing much, except maybe a couple of us stationed around the cabin noticed a bit of a light show happening a few times. It was mostly just light from the bedroom window and a few stray sparks that seemed harmless enough. No real energy behind them. No destructive intent. Just pretty special effects, which is what we've decided to call them since there's a movie star involved." Mario was chuckling, now, and Nick just shook his head.

"Do me a favor and ask everybody to keep that to themselves. I don't want you guys embarrassing her. She's just barely convinced that all magic isn't evil. I'd like to give her a chance to explore her power without being self-conscious about it because of you guys."

Mario sobered. "Come on, Nick. You know we wouldn't do anything to embarrass the lady. We like her."

"You do?" Nick was surprised. He hadn't expected his people to accept Sal so quickly. They were usually much more wary than that.

"Hell, any woman who can get the mighty Nick Balam to

let his guard down has to be pretty special. We all took a vote, and if she's your mate—which I think is a pretty sure bet after the way you answered the door just now—then we're all for it." Mario's tone grew more serious. "We want you to be happy, Nick."

Nick didn't know how to respond, and frankly, he got a little choked up at the idea that his people cared so much for his happiness. He hadn't ever thought about it before, but he should have realized they cared for him as much as he cared for every single one of them. They had worked closely together for a long time, and bonds of friendship had built up between them all.

Something warm unfurled in his heart as he realized all this, and he gave Mario a solemn nod, unable to speak for a moment. Apparently, no words needed to be said. Mario came over, gave Nick a back-pounding hug, and then headed for the door.

"Oh, by the way, Mr. Howell is planning to come over after breakfast to give your lady another magic lesson. You might want to eat up and get dressed so you don't have to answer the door wearing a wrinkled sheet again."

Nick could hear Mario's laughter long after the door shut behind him.

CHAPTER 14

Though disappointed not to be able to share a leisurely awakening with her new lover, Sal rose to the challenge when Nick woke her with a steaming cup of tea and a sweet kiss. He told her about the waiting breakfast and imminent visit from her new magic teacher, and she found the motivation to get out of bed and into the shower.

They were just finishing breakfast when Nick went to open the door. Somehow, he'd heard the approach of the off-road vehicle carrying Mr. Howell long before Sal had. She had time to clear the table and pack up the used dishes while Nick welcomed the older man and ushered him into the cabin.

Sal exchanged greetings with Mr. Howell while Nick gathered the used items into the picnic basket. He hefted it as he headed for the door.

"Unless you need me for something," Nick said, "I'm going to go out for a bit. Mario will be nearby if you need anything and he knows how to reach me."

Howell waved him on. "Go ahead, young man. We'll be fine for a couple of hours."

Nick winked at Sal, and then, he was gone. She turned to look at Mr. Howell, and he smiled at her.

"You two make a nice couple," he told her, making her

cheeks heat with a blush.

Nick gave the used breakfast dishes in the basket to Mario and left him with instructions to keep an eye on things. Nick peeled off into the jungle, stashing his clothing at the base of a window on the side of the cabin while he let his jaguar run.

His inner cat needed to prowl the territory and sniff out any possible threats to its mate. In his cat form, his nose was much more sensitive, and he could almost smell the faintly ozone-like smell of magic coming from the cabin where his mate studied with the mage master. Nick realized once again how lucky they had been to have Howell staying on the island just when Sal needed him most.

Nick had always been taught that the Mother of All worked in mysterious ways, and now, he was a true believer. Howell might be there because his daughter had just become the Alpha's mate and discovered her own magic that had lain dormant all her life, but he was also there to help Sal, which meant more to Nick than he could put into words. Without Howell and his skills, who knew what might have happened when Sal's rogue magic awoke?

All she'd known of magic all her life had been turmoil and madness. With her only example that of her poor mother, the outcome could have been disastrous. Instead, Howell was here to gently teach her that magic wasn't necessarily evil. He'd been able to show her another way. A better way. A way to live with, and control, the power that was her birthright.

But what were the odds that both Mark and Nick would find mates with hidden magic? They'd laid the groundwork for rebuilding the Clan here on Jaguar Island, but it would still take generations to increase their numbers, and during that time, they remained vulnerable, even here in what would become the Clan stronghold. Maybe the Mother of All was sending Her support in the form of these powerful women who could take their places at the heart of the Clan.

Shelly was already doing great things, designing community buildings and homes for their people that would be built over the next few years. She'd been welcomed as Alpha female, mate to their leader. And she'd already shown she had a kind heart and generous spirit. Would the Clan take as readily to Sal as they had to Shelly? Nick wasn't sure, but the response of his security team—relayed through Mario— gave him hope.

He prowled the perimeter, his cat glad to have the freedom to run, climb and sniff to its hearts content. He'd been forced to stay in human form a bit longer than he'd liked while on this mission, but he was safe to be who he was here on the island. He ran through the jungle, jumping over obstacles and pausing here and there to check the scents left behind by his patrols. He was well satisfied they were doing their jobs, guarding the cabin as he'd asked.

Then, it was time to go back. He found a new spring in his steps as he headed back to the cabin, eager to see her again. His mate. The cat purred in satisfaction. Finally, both sides of his soul knew the truth of it. Sal was theirs, and they would never let her go.

Sal was alone in the cabin when he returned, so he didn't bother shifting back. He wanted to see her reaction to his cat form, now that things were quiet and there was no danger to sidetrack them. She'd seemed okay with him when he'd done the half-shift in front of her at the apartment in California, but he wanted to make sure she was okay with his fully feline form. The cat needed her approval, vain thing that it was.

Luckily, the door was unlocked, and the handle was made so that paws could open it. He jumped up, leaning one paw on the doorframe, the other working the handle and then pushing inward once the door unlatched. He paused, leaning his weight on the one paw that was on the frame, to look inside.

He found Sal sitting on the couch, and she must've heard the door open because she turned to meet his gaze. Her eyes widened as they met his, but she didn't jump or scream.

"Nick?" she asked, uncertainty in her voice.

His cat form didn't like that she couldn't tell him apart

from other jaguars, but he'd fix that once she acknowledged their mating. She'd learn the unique pattern of his spots and the distinctive shape and size of him. That would start now. But, first, she needed to know it was him.

He nodded his head, his whiskers brushing the doorframe in an annoying way. He saw her expression change. She had understood his gesture. Good.

Nick pushed off that one paw and allowed himself to flow to the ground. He entered the cabin then used one back foot to close the door behind him. He deliberately let his claws make a little noise on the wooden floor so she'd know where he was. The last thing he wanted to do was frighten his mate, but the cat side needed her acceptance, too. She had to be able to deal with both of his forms.

Sal felt a bit apprehensive, knowing she was in an enclosed space with a fierce jungle cat that had to weigh a few hundred pounds. She knew it was Nick, of course, but there was still some primal fear at being caged with an apex predator. Then, he slunk closer, his golden eyes meeting hers. She could see the magic swirling within his gaze.

Strangely, seeing it there calmed her rather than ratcheting up her fear. Since learning a little bit about magic and how to control it, she could see the very carefully reined-in magic that was part of Nick's soul. He had complete control over the magic that made him what he was. It didn't rule him, he ruled it.

That was the very significant difference between him—as well as the others she'd met, like Mr. Howell and Collin Hastings—and her mother. When the wild magic came for her mom, it was completely out of control. Her mother didn't have the skills or knowledge of what to do to rein it in. Not like Nick and the others. Not like the jungle cat that walked in front of her and stood there, watching her with Nick's magical eyes.

She was seated on the couch, and he had padded into the space between the couch and the small wooden coffee table in front of it. He moved silently now that he was walking on the rug that filled the conversation area where the couch and two armchairs were located in front of the fireplace.

He walked right up to her side and then sat on his haunches, just looking at her, waiting for her reaction, she reasoned. Feeling her fear subside as he made no aggressive moves, she looked at him.

"You're gorgeous, Nick," she whispered, mesmerized by the pattern of his spots. His fur was a living, breathing work of art, and it looked really soft. "Is it okay if I touch you?"

In answer, he moved his head closer to her lap, putting his chin on her knee and tilting toward the hand she had left on her thigh. Well, he couldn't be much clearer than that, she thought. Sal reached out to stroke his neck, enthralled by the incredible luxury of his silky coat.

"So soft," she whispered, digging her fingers in as he seemed to enjoy her stroking.

Little sparkles of magical energy followed the path of her fingers over his fur. Nothing harmful. Just the little tickle of magic that seemed to flare between them now whenever they touched. It was visible against the dark marks on his fur and gave her something else to marvel at while she became fully enchanted with this new side of her lover.

They hadn't really had any time to themselves since their momentous change in status. Sal thought she knew where she stood with him, but sometimes, a gal needed the reassurance of words. Not that he'd be able to say much in his current form. No, The Talk would have to wait until he shifted back to the form that spoke instead of growled and purred. Though, come to think of it, he purred pretty well in his human form, too.

Maybe she could say a few things, right now, that she wouldn't have the courage to say to his human face? Sometimes, a captive audience that didn't talk back made it easier to open up. It was worth a try. She had been wanting to tell him a few things since last night but found it difficult to talk about her past or her feelings. She might be a movie star now, with her life on public view, but that was all for show.

The real Sal was hidden behind so many layers of protection she seldom saw the light of day. Then, Nick had come into her life and started peeling away at her shells. He'd gotten right down to the heart of her in no time flat, and while she liked the results, she still felt a little fragile. The whole experience—though ultimately a good one—had been somewhat traumatic in the process.

"Nick…" she began, searching for courage. "About last night."

Oh, yeah, she had his full attention now. He went from pussycat to alert predator under her trailing fingers. She wasn't afraid of him. She knew deep in her heart that he would never hurt her. She was more afraid of her feelings and what he might do next…and whether she could survive with her soul intact if he turned away from her now.

"First, I want you to know, I enjoyed everything we did together and would like to continue exploring this…relationship…if you want that, too." Had she imagined his sleek muscles relaxing under her hand? The magic swirl of energy in his eyes calmed a little but still held strong as he looked at her. "I just want to make sure we're both on the same page here. I know you still have your doubts about me, and I can't really blame you for that. I just hope that, from here on, we can begin again. I'm willing to learn about your world—about magic—now that I've seen a few things that have begun to change my opinion about magic in general. I'm willing to meet you halfway on the subject of magic. I hope you'll consider forgiving me for the secrets I kept from you. I didn't do it to purposely deceive you." She looked down, breaking eye contact, feeling extremely vulnerable.

A shimmer in the air, and under her hand, Nick's shoulder went from furry to firm, muscular, and all too human. She looked upward to find him kneeling in front of her, naked as the day he was born.

Yum, was her first uncensored thought, followed quickly by, *Down, girl.*

"I know you didn't, Sal. I figured that you were just doing the best you could to protect yourself. I've done a lot of thinking about your past—now that I know the truth of it—and I've come to some conclusions. We all have, in fact."

"Mark knows everything," she said.

"Yes," he agreed. "And you can bet that you're the topic of conversation up at the big house. Decisions are being made, I'm sure. What they'll be, I can guess...but I can't be certain until we see what happens. In the meantime, I'm here. With you. Where I want to be."

He moved in on her then, coming closer. Where she wanted him to be, too. Forget what might happen later. What she wanted right now was on offer, and she'd be a fool to turn him away. Not when she knew how good they were together and especially not when she had no idea what the future would bring.

She would grab the brass ring while it was within reach and let the chips fall where they may later. For now, she was with her lover, and she wanted to be *with* him again. As often as she could.

Sal launched herself at him and took him down to the floor, covering his nude body with her, sadly, clothed self. But they'd fix that soon enough. She straddled his hips and lifted up to pull her top eagerly over her head while Nick's hands went to the clasp of her bra. It came away in short order, the fabric cups to be replaced by his warm hands.

Mmm. That felt wonderful. Especially when he started playing with the sensitive peaks. While he did that, she struggled out of her pants and panties, her desire riding her hard.

Speaking of hard, he was solid and long beneath her, and as ready for action as she was quickly becoming. This wouldn't be a long, drawn-out affair. No, this was needy, quick, powerful sex with the man she could so easily become addicted to. This was raw. It was soul-wrenching. It was real.

As real as anything had ever been in her difficult life. She'd gone into acting to hide in fantasy, to continue playing roles—and she had for so many years. Turning a survival skill she had developed into a career.

But now, with Nick, all her subterfuge was gone. She could be the real Sal—whoever that was—with him. That was a gift greater than any she had ever received, and he'd been the one to give it to her. With him, she could be the sex-starved wild woman that reigned, right now, or she could be the student wanting to know the realities of magic, like she was with Mr. Howell. She could allow the true facets of her innermost nature to show and have no fear that it would come back to haunt her.

Nick would never hurt her. Not in any way.

And with that stunning realization, she took him into her body, seating herself on him, moaning at the contact that meant everything...or nothing...depending on the outcome of those discussions currently ongoing at the mansion.

Knowing her future happiness hung on the balance of conversations she was not even allowed to be part of, she decided to ignore the possible outcomes and just enjoy the moment. This moment. Right here. Nick and Sal, on the floor of a jungle cabin. No lies between them. No dreams of the future. No nightmares of the past. Just now and this incredible attraction they shared.

She moved on him urgently, wanting this moment to last a lifetime. Craving so much more than she could have—at least not until her fate and position with regards to the Clan were settled. She wanted a future with the man beneath her. She wanted a life filled with his loving, his companionship, his...love.

Dare she want it all? Love was dangerous. She loved her mother but had been unable to protect her and save her from herself when the wild magic came to call. Sal had done all she could to help, while her own heart bled at her mother's situation.

All she knew of love was desperation and pain, but with Nick... Nick showed her possibilities. He let her dream of how things could be. With him.

It was a dangerous dream. It made her want a future with him. But did he feel the same way?

The question was too complicated for the moment. The only thing that mattered right here, right now, was their bodies straining together, reaching for oblivion where they were no longer separate beings, but two hearts, beating as one.

Her movements became erratic as her pleasure soared higher. She had her hands on his chest, supporting her as she leaned upward. The slight change in angle sent her to the stars, and she was dimly aware of Nick joining her as he shouted her name, his hands clasping her hips hard, holding her to him as they went together on a trip neither could take alone.

CHAPTER 15

A long time later, Nick was still breathing hard. So was Sal. His beautiful Sal. Lying atop him like a warm, ultra-feminine blanket. He would stay just like that the rest of the day—hell, the rest of his *life*—if he could, but reality intruded.

His sensitive ears picked up the sound of an engine working its way up the drive toward the cabin. They'd be here in minutes, and he knew Sal wouldn't want to be caught in a compromising situation like this. It was bad enough his people knew they'd bunked together last night. Though they would never deliberately hurt her, they wouldn't mind teasing the hell out of him, which, if she heard it, would embarrass her. He didn't want that.

He wanted to protect her from everything, including embarrassment, which technically couldn't really hurt her, but his cat was in super high gear when it came to protecting its mate. He wanted her life to be without trouble of any kind from here on, out and he'd do his utmost to make sure that happened.

Nick rose to a sitting position on the floor. They were sort of lodged between the couch and the coffee table, with just enough room to maneuver, but Sal was still kind of out of it. Manly pride puffed out his chest. He'd loved her into a stupor. *Grr.* Kitty liked that.

Working his way up from the floor with her in his arms, he padded barefoot, and bare-assed, into his bedroom. He tucked her into the bed where she promptly rolled over and hugged his pillow to her chest, dropping off into a doze with a smile on her face. Damn. He liked her reaction to making love with him.

Grabbing some clothes on his way out of the room, he threw them on just as the vehicle rolled to a stop in front of the cabin. Nick went out to meet the lunch delivery and sent them on their way just as quickly. He didn't want anything to disturb his mate. He'd let her sleep for a bit, then they'd share a leisurely lunch while he waited to see what might happen next.

They got to have their lunch together and were just cleaning up the remnants when another vehicle approached. Surprised, Nick went to the door to see who their afternoon visitor might be. He was only mildly surprised to find that Abuela had come herself to check out the new arrival. He'd half-expected the Clan's healer and everyone's grandmother—either by blood or by friendship—to come up here, even though she was one of the oldest members of the Clan and didn't like to travel too far from the comforts of the mansion these days.

She got her old bones out of the Jeep, which had been driven by a younger Clan member who stayed outside when Nick invited his grandmother in. She gave him a big hug, which he dutifully bent down to receive. When she released him, her smile lit his heart, as it had done since he'd been a little boy.

"Introduce me to your girl," Abuela said, grinning, and Nick knew it would be all right. His grandmother might be scary to some, but she'd always been a pussycat when it came to him.

"Sal, this is my grandmother. Abuela, this is Sal, my mate."

Sal was a little surprised by his words, but she didn't make a fuss. Not when his grandmother was standing there, waiting for Sal to say something. Instead, she gave the older woman her best smile and moved closer with her hand held out in what she hoped would be seen as a friendly gesture. She wanted to make a good impression. It was clear Nick loved this old woman and that her opinion probably meant a lot to him.

"It's a pleasure to meet you, ma'am," she said politely as Abuela took her hand...and didn't let go.

The old woman grasped Sal's hand in both of hers then tilted her head back and closed her eyes. Sal sent Nick a questioning look, but he was watching his grandmother intently. Was Sal being measured in some strange way? It sure looked like it.

Suddenly more nervous than before, she felt a small trickle of magic tingle along her arm and into her hand. Sal panicked, doing her best to stop the magic. She didn't want to hurt Nick's grandmother or let wild magic take over, but Sal was powerless to stop the small flow of magic from her hand into Abuela's hard grip.

Then, the old lady smiled and opened her eyes, and the magic stopped.

"Strong, this one," Abuela said to Nick, as if in approval.

Sal's breath caught at the swirling golden magic in the old woman's eyes. This little old lady was powerful. She was a shifter, yes, but she was more than that. Much more. And how Sal knew that little tidbit, she really had no idea.

"Like recognizes like," Abuela said, chuckling as she let go of Sal's hand. "You see with the eyes of a mage-born, though I have talked at length with Master Howell about you, and it's clear your education needs some work."

Sal tried not to let her embarrassment show on her face, but she felt about an inch tall at the old woman's light scolding. Any number of defensive words came to mind, but she bit them back. She sensed that this little old woman wouldn't accept any excuses for not having trained her magical power—even though it had only just decided to show up.

Sal had lived in denial most of her life. It was a huge adjustment to go from a girl with good instincts but no visible magic to someone who could hold fireballs in her hand. She still could hardly believe she'd done that. Multiple times, too. Mr. Howell had insisted she learn basic control and suggested that was one of the better ways since it produced a visible phenomenon she could both see and feel.

Apparently, not all magic was like that, and Sal knew she had a hell of a lot to learn. Coming to it so late in life, she would probably be spending a lot of time catching up on basic skills usually taught to children who grew up in a family of mages. At least, that's what Mr. Howell had explained to her.

He'd also told her that his own daughter hadn't been raised that way. Like Sal, his daughter's magic had been latent all her life, and he'd made the decision to protect her rather than have her grow up with full knowledge of the world she could never be part of. He'd distanced himself from his daughter, working in the shadows to keep her safe from the family's enemies.

But everything had changed when his daughter arrived on the island in the company of the jaguar Alpha. Mr. Howell had shaken his head, seeming to still be surprised by the idea that his little girl was now mated to one of the richest and most powerful men in the country, if not the world. And that surprising union had finally given his daughter access to the magic that was her family's birthright.

Mr. Howell had even hinted that perhaps his daughter, Shelly, would benefit from training with Sal. They were both novices when it came to their understanding of magic, but they were also both adults with full-grown powers.

Sal was still trying to wrap her head around everything Mr. Howell had told her. And now, this. Nick had sprung his grandmother on her without any warning. If Sal had known she would be meeting his family, she would have tried to prepare herself. Maybe run a brush through her hair or slap on some lipstick or something. Instead, Abuela had caught her totally off guard.

"Master Howell said you were a quick study," Nick's grandmother went on, seemingly unaware of Sal's internal turmoil. "He claims you can control your fire. Is that not so?"

The old woman seemed to be daring Sal. Challenging her. Pushing her to display the few things she had learned. A desire to prove herself to this woman rose in Sal's gut, and she held out her hand, allowing a small ball of fire to develop in her palm, just the way Mr. Howell had shown her. She let it grow, holding it steady as it began to light the room and spread its gentle heat toward her, then she commanded it to dissipate, going back from whence it had come…and it responded to her desires. It did just as she asked.

That still amazed her. It probably would always amaze her. All her life, Sal had lived with the fear of wild magic rising in her soul. Well, the magic had come, but it wasn't exactly wild. Not the way it was with her mother. Not since Mr. Howell had taken Sal in hand.

Sal had hope that she might live through this, essentially intact. There was no doubt she would have a lot more knowledge, and perhaps a new set of skills, but she wouldn't wind up like her mother. For the first time, she had hope that she could live with this curse, though Mr. Howell insisted on calling it a gift.

Abuela was beaming at her when Sal dismissed the fireball and looked into the old woman's eyes. Sal read approval in that ancient gaze. Approval and respect. Wow.

"I've seen enough. You two should not stay way out here all alone. I want you both to come to the big house. It will be easier for Master Howell and I to see to your education if we're all staying in the same place." Nick's grandmother turned to him. "Unless you have another reason for wanting to be alone." Those old eyes showed sparkles of mirth as she teased her grandson.

"That's none of your business, Abuela," Nick growled, but with clear love in every word.

"It is my business. I want great-grandchildren, Nicky. I'm not getting any younger here." Laughter accompanied her teasing words, and Sal felt her cheeks heat at the idea of providing those great-grandchildren…and just how they might be conceived.

And just like that, it was decided that Sal's exile to the cabin was over, and she was welcome among the rest of the Clan. Nick wasn't sure exactly how to feel about that. On the one hand, he wanted his mate to be accepted among his people. On the other, he really liked being alone with her in the middle of nowhere.

Abuela sent him outside so that she could spend some time with Sal, teaching her more about magic and how to control it. Nick cooled his heels, walking the perimeter and checking in with his sentries. All was well, but he knew Abuela would want more time to work with and assess Sal. Some unnamed fear kept him close to the cabin. He couldn't just leave two of the most important women in his life alone and not stay within reach should they need him.

So, he paced. And prowled. And just walked around, checking and rechecking the local area. Mostly, he was just trying to burn off his own nervous energy, but it wasn't really working.

At length, Abuela opened the door to the cabin and came outside. Nick walked over to meet her as she made her way toward her car, which had waited for her, the youngster behind the wheel having passed the time playing games on her phone. She wasn't on the security team. Heck, she wasn't even old enough to legally drive had they been on the mainland.

The girl was Abuela's little helper, which meant she accompanied Grandmother wherever she went and did whatever she asked the girl to do. Nick thought of her as a personal assistant—though a very young one. Abuela liked to work with the younger members of the Clan, teaching them by showing them kindness and including them in her important work. She cycled through the youngsters on a regular basis, making sure to spread her influence and love around wherever it was needed most.

This girl was new to the personal assistant position, but she would learn to pay more attention to her surroundings eventually. Nick didn't take her to task because this was the only place on Earth right now where jaguars could go about their business without looking over their shoulders every single minute. He wouldn't ruin that for the youngster.

Nick met his grandmother halfway to the waiting vehicle, just out of earshot of the game-playing pre-teen. He could see Sal closing the door behind Abuela, a soft smile on her face. He took that to mean the visit had gone well.

"Nicky, you are a foolish man." Abuela wasn't mincing words as she put her hand on her grandson's shoulder. "There isn't an evil bone in that girl's body. Anybody could see that."

"I know, I know," he tried to placate her. "But I thought she had lied to me when the magic suddenly appeared. She didn't tell me about her past and the many skeletons in her closet." He was still mad that she hadn't trusted him with the secret of her mother's incarceration.

"And how many of your secrets did you tell her?" Abuela challenged. "A few, certainly," the old woman allowed. "But not all. Not everything. You have not divulged every little bit of your past to her. You may never do so, and you would be within your rights. As she was within her rights to keep the painful secret about her mother. You two have only just met. You are mates, but you are new to it, and it will take time to develop the trust that comes with years. You are too impatient. Too quick to judge. How could you ever believe for a single moment that your mate might hold evil in her heart?"

Abuela was truly angry with him now. Her voice was shaking, and the hand on his shoulder rose to slap his cheek lightly.

"Stupid boy. The Mother of All would never allow that.

She would not mate you—Beta and protector of our Clan—with an evil woman. You should have had more faith." Abuela's disappointment was written all over her lined face and made Nick feel about two inches tall.

"I'm sorry, Abuela," he whispered, knowing she was right to have called him on his bullshit.

"It's not me you need to apologize to. Your mate is in there, and she needs your faith in her now more than ever. She needs your unconditional love and unquestioning loyalty." Abuela pointed toward the cabin. "And you need to make your peace with the Goddess, too. You doubted Her wisdom, and you, of all shifters, should know She has plans for us that aren't always clear, but that always work out for the best. She moves in mysterious ways, and it is for us to have faith and believe that She is doing the best for us. How could you have forgotten that? My own grandson?" Abuela's eyebrows rose as she regarded him for a long moment, then she relented. "You must begin to teach your mate more about our ways. If she's going to be part of our Clan, she will need such knowledge."

"Is she going to be part of the Clan?" There it was. Nick's biggest worry. He'd already decided he would leave the Clan and his responsibilities behind, if they couldn't accept Sal. She was his mate. She had to come first.

"That's up to you," Abuela said, stepping back. "And her." Abuela looked back at the cabin for a moment then sighed. "And the Alpha." She started walking toward her vehicle, and Nick fell into step beside her. "For my part, I will advise the Alpha to accept her. She is a good woman, and the Mother of All has sent her to us for a reason."

"You really think so?" he couldn't help but ask, risking his grandmother's renewed wrath.

"Nicky." She shook her head slowly, clearly disappointed that he still questioned. "Don't you think it's quite a coincidence that both the Alpha and Beta have found mates who were latent mages until they came to our island? *Two* women of great power, unused to the ways of magic. Mages unknown to magical circles. Mages bound by love to our Clan for all time. I don't believe that is an accident. I think, rather, it is a gift from the Goddess we all serve. Two strong mages to help us in our time of rebuilding, to share their power with their children and our Clan, to make us stronger in the future. We should not fear these women. We should welcome them with open arms, like the gifts they are."

Put that way, Nick could hardly keep arguing. Abuela was a wise woman of the Clan. A healer and medicine woman. Before Mr. Howell had shown up to help his daughter train her newfound magic, Abuela had been the one helping Shelly. Grandmother had always been a bit more magical than others in the Clan. As was her entire bloodline. Nick included.

She'd given him a great deal to think about, his mind whirring even as he helped his grandmother into the waiting vehicle. The pre-teen at the wheel finally put away her phone and started the engine. They were gone a moment later.

His head was spinning, but he knew one thing—he had to talk to Sal. He headed for the cabin, entering quietly to find Sal standing near the doorway, hands on hips, in what looked to be a fine temper.

"What did you mean when you said I was your mate?" she asked without preamble.

Nick immediately paused his steps. Abuela had been so right. He'd dug a hole for himself with his mate, and it would be up to him to dig himself right back out. But he had to do this delicately. He had one shot here, and he didn't want to blow it.

"Shifters are a bit different from everybody else," he began, drawing a shake of her head and a hint of a smile from her lips. Good. She wasn't set rock solid against him. She was listening.

"You can say that again," she allowed, leaning back to rest her shapely butt against the back of the couch, her arms folded as she waited for him to explain.

"Yeah, well, that goes for the way we find our mates, too. See, we believe in the Goddess. The Mother of All. We believe She sets us on a path that will help us find our perfect mate. It's a bit different than for humans. With shifters, mates are strictly one per customer. We don't divorce. We don't fall in and out of love, like I've seen so many humans do. When we mate, it's for life."

He held her gaze, even as she stood from her leaning position, tension in her stance as her eyes widened.

"And you..." She seemed to be having trouble speaking. She cleared her throat and tried again. "You think *I'm*...your perfect mate?"

Nick advanced on her, slowly stalking closer, holding her startled gaze. Startled was good. Fear was not. The moment he saw fear in her eyes, he'd back off, but for right now, he found hope blossoming in his heart. So far, she was handling this as well as could be expected.

"I suspected it almost from the first moment we met," he admitted softly. "But I was fighting it. I sensed you were keeping secrets from me, and there was the safety of the Clan to consider. You'd seen a shift. You might've had evidence. You could have been an enemy—or even just a misguided soul seeking to profit from the news about shifters. I had to be wary. And I regret my wariness and suspicion almost ruined everything." He shook his head, concerned that he could still botch this. "But through it all, there was this undeniable attraction. A pull from my soul to yours. A bond that was forming no matter how much in denial I was."

He stalked closer with each word until he was only inches from her, holding her gaze as if his life depended on it. And maybe—just maybe—it did.

"Do you feel it, too?" he asked the final question. The one that would make or break this whole shebang. Then, he waited, apprehensive of her answer.

CHAPTER 16

Sal thought about his words, and the way he was laying it all on the line here. That took courage. She recognized her power in that moment—the power to crush his hopes or make both of their dreams come true—and she couldn't deny him.

"I feel it, Nick," she admitted in a shaky voice. "It's like a magnet, drawing me to you."

"And me to you," he agreed, hope shining in his eyes.

"It all happened so fast," she breathed as he drew closer, his head dropping down toward hers.

"That's the way it is with shifters. We fall hard, and we fall fast. And we love forever." He nibbled on her lips, and she almost let the moment carry her away. Almost.

Hands on his chest, she pushed gently, to make some space between them. She looked up into his eyes, the moment more important than any other moment in her life.

"You love me?" she asked, trying desperately to settle the small hint of fear still in the pit of her stomach.

Were they too different to make a go of this? Were shifters meant to be with humans? Or even human mages who hadn't known they were mages until very recently? The thoughts jumbled through her mind, making little sense...except for the fear that she might still lose him, somehow, despite his words. Perhaps it was fear of belief. If she believed in him and then he left, she knew she would never survive.

But Nick held her gaze, the magic swirling slowly in his eyes, his expression as serious as she'd ever seen it. Hope started to overshadow the fear in her heart.

"I love you, Sal. I will always love you, and I will never leave you unless you drive me away. Even then, I'll watch over you from afar, if that's all I have left. When shifters mate, it's forever. I'm afraid you're stuck with me, sweetheart." At last, he smiled, and it was as if the sun had come out after months of rain. *Years* of rain, in her case.

She could deny the joy in her heart no more.

"I love you, too, Nick," she told him, smiling as he did. "It's all happened so fast, but I feel it in my heart. In my soul. I love you, and I never want us to be apart."

Now, it was his turn to beam at her, tugging her into his arms for a jubilant embrace. He lifted her high and twirled her around the room, making her feel carefree in a way that she hadn't felt for a very long time. Breathless, she hugged him back, wanting the moment of mutual discovery to go on and on.

He slowed them, looking down into her eyes as he let her feet touch the ground. "It's fast, but it's real, Sal. As real as anything has ever been."

She caught her breath, feeling the magic rise and meet his, touching, exploring, not out of her control but definitely doing its own thing. He seemed to feel it, too.

"I have another little confession to make," he told her somewhat sheepishly. "Being part of the Balam bloodline means I have a little more magic than most jaguars. I guess that's why it bothered me so much that I hadn't detected your magic. I'm sorry, Sal. The extra dose of magic is what makes me Beta and protector of the Clan and why my grandma is a wise woman. Somewhere in our family tree is a mage—or maybe more than just one—and that gives us a little extra something."

"That's why my magic reaches out to you," she reasoned,

and he nodded.

"Yeah, probably. But we can ask Abuela, if you want. She knows more about it than I do, that's for sure. My strength is more martial than magical." He settled his arms around her waist, looking at her with a speculative gaze that held a bit of humor. "I suspect any children we manage to have will be quite a handful, and probably a lot more magical than their old man."

Children? She gulped, already dreaming about what they would be like. She'd never thought she'd have children because she'd feared passing on the curse of wild magic, but now... Now, everything was different. She had hope for the future, and with Nick, children were not only possible but very much desired.

"I think I'm really going to like being mated to you," she told him, only partly joking. Nick had changed her whole world. For the better.

Nick growled and picked her up, taking her to his bedroom and laying her down on the big bed. She didn't argue. She wanted to make love to him, right now, more than she wanted her next breath.

They undressed each other with eager hands, getting down to skin on skin in record time. Then, there was a slight pause as they kissed and stroked each other to new levels of yearning, driving each other up the ramp of passion toward their ultimate goal. Sal gave as good as she got and felt a thrill race down her spine when he started that sexy low purring that seemed to come to him at times like these.

Yeah, that was a total turn on. His rumbling chest against hers was all kinds of sexy and made her eager for more. She climbed on top of him and let him know in no uncertain terms what she wanted. Taking when he gave and joining them with gusto when he might've held back.

Then, she began to ride him. Slow, at first, her strokes became more intense, more fluid, more impatient as she went along. Her passion rose and rose...and then rose some more, reaching toward a height that only Nick had ever shown her.

And then, the magic began to rise, as well, and for a moment, she faltered.

But it was cool. She was in control. The magic wasn't running away from her to do God-only-knew-what. It was running toward Nick, and he was meeting it. Caressing it. Like he caressed her body with his hands. Somehow, his magic was accepting hers and returning the tingling stroke for stroke.

Her breath caught at the sensations—both physical and magical. Who knew sex could be so multi-dimensional?

Aware of her now as never before, Nick could feel Sal's magic reaching toward his, touching tentatively at first, then twining together with his, as if they had been made for each other. They had been, after all. He and Sal had been matched up by the Goddess. They were mates. It wasn't all that surprising—or at least it shouldn't have been—that their innate powers would recognize each other and blend together.

The flavor of her power was quite different from his. She wasn't a shifter, for one thing. That was a huge difference right there. But they were more alike than he had imagined. Given the chance for their energies to intertwine as their bodies came together in passion, the magic roiled and bubbled happily—not at all contentiously. This was a good match. One that would stand the test of time...and beyond.

As Nick and Sal made love on the physical plane, their powers came to terms with each other on the magical and spiritual planes. There was a joining, and a blending, that resulted in a new incarnation for each of them. They came together as separate beings and came out of the encounter joined. Renewed. Reenergized. Remade.

When their bodies reached for the ultimate reward, together, the magic poured out, sparkling around them together, an echo of what their bodies were doing. Climax after climax was powered by both the physical and the magical, lasting long after any previous experience Nick had ever had with other women.

There were no other women. Not anymore. From now on, the only woman he could contemplate was his mate. His perfect match. His Goddess-given joy.

"I love you, Sal," he whispered in her ear as they clung together, magic swirling around them.

He felt her relax into him. "I love you, too, Nick. With all my heart."

*

As the sun set, Nick pulled up in the driveway of the mansion on the other side of the island. Sal was beside him, as he hoped she would be for the rest of their lives. What came next would determine whether he—whether *they*—would stay here as part of the Jaguar Clan or have to move on. Mark would have to make a decision to either accept Sal into the Clan or lose Nick forever. It was just that simple. And that scary.

Nick got out of the Jeep and tossed the keys to a nearby youngster whose job it was to keep the drive clear. He'd park the Jeep around back, out of sight, with the other vehicles as soon as Nick escorted his new mate into the mansion. The kid would also unload their bags and put them in Nick's room, so Nick was unencumbered as he offered Sal his arm and led her up to the doorway.

The door was thrown open before they got there, the new Alpha female offering a cheery welcome to Sal, and a somewhat suspicious look thrown toward Nick. Shelly still hadn't forgiven him for interrogating her when they'd first met, but he figured she'd give up her mad in a few months...or, maybe years. Possibly.

"I'm Shelly Howell...uh...Pepard. Sorry, that's still kind of new to me." Shelly's open smile invited all around to join in. She had a naturally sunny personality that had only gotten brighter since her mating. "My dad's been telling me all about you, Miss Lane."

Sal offered her hand and returned Shelly's smile. "Oh, please, call me Sal. Your dad's been helping me a lot. He's a really great guy. And congratulations on your marriage." Sal was making small talk, offering all the right noises as the two women moved into the foyer of the big house.

Nick was aware of Mark standing at the back of the open space, watching his mate and the newcomers. The fact that he'd let his mate come forward on her own to greet Sal was a good sign. It showed a level of trust Nick, quite frankly, hadn't expected so soon.

Maybe... Maybe the trust wasn't for Sal, per se, but more for Nick's judgment. After so many years growing up together, working together, and facing danger together, Mark and Nick had formed a friendship based on mutual respect. Up 'til now, Mark had trusted Nick to watch his back in many different types of dangerous situations. Perhaps that had earned Nick a bit of leeway when it came to introducing an unknown into the Clan.

Though, really, after spending time with Howell and passing Abuela's tests—whatever they had been—Sal wasn't really that much of an unknown anymore. Oh, she probably still had a few surprises in store, but Nick knew deep in his heart that his mate could never pose a real threat to anyone he loved. Mark and his mate were part of that select group.

Nick caught Mark's eye, and the Alpha nodded, moving smoothly forward to intercept the women. Nick made the introductions.

"Sal, this is Mark Pepard." Nick watched as she reached forward to take the Alpha's hand, each of them taking careful stock of each other.

"Welcome to Jaguar Island, Miss Lane," Mark said, pouring on the charm as Nick breathed a sigh of relief.

"Please, call me Sal."

"I thought the newspapers all called you Sully?" Shelly asked.

"They do, but...that just doesn't feel right. I was born Sally Lannier. I only became Sully Lane recently, and only the newspapers and a few of the people I work with call me that. Somehow, when I met Nick, it didn't feel appropriate to hide behind the stage name. The only one who still calls me Sal is my mom," Sal's voice dropped into a sad tone. "And now, you guys."

"I'm honored," Mark replied, equally somber. He seemed to understand the importance of what Sal was telling them.

For his part, Nick was blown away by the fact that she'd been following her instincts since the moment they met and she'd asked him to call her by the name only her mother still used. That meant something to him. It was a clear indication that the Goddess did, indeed, move in mysterious ways, and that his mate had known, on some instinctual level, when they met that there was something special happening. Nick's inner cat wanted to purr in both triumph and satisfaction.

"We were just about to head in for dinner. Do you guys need to freshen up or are you good to go?" Shelly asked.

Sal looked at Nick, shrugging. "I'm kind of hungry," she offered, letting him decide for both of them.

"I could eat, thanks," Nick said. "We'll head in with you."

And just like that, the two couples were walking together through the large house, heading for the far dining room and the Clan members already gathered there. One hurdle jumped, and things were starting to look really good for the future. Nick started to breathe a little easier, though he was still on guard. Mark had to give his formal welcome—accepting Sal into the Clan—before they would be home free.

"Where's your dad?" Nick asked Shelly as they walked.

"He flew out to California this afternoon, to meet Sal's mother," she replied almost offhandedly, though she had to know how big this news was. "My dad's been known to commit the odd philanthropic gesture. This move could be made to fit into that scenario because, though I was kept in the dark for a long time, apparently, my father has done this sort of thing before—rescuing mages who've had little or no training and helping them learn control."

Beside him, Sal's steps faltered, and she grabbed for Nick's hand. Mark and Shelly stopped walking and turned to face Nick and Sal. Mark eyed them both.

"I'm looking into your mother's case," he told Sal directly. "There's a good chance I'll be able to pull some strings and get her released into Mr. Howell's care. He's got a foundation already set up that has done this sort of thing before, oddly enough." Mark smiled and shook his head as if he was surprised by the turn of events himself. "Eventually, if you're agreeable, and depending on my father-in-law's recommendation, I wouldn't be opposed to moving your mother to the island so she could continue learning how to control her wild magic. At least here, her chances of hurting anyone are greatly diminished, even if her magic goes out of control again."

"Really?" Sal looked like she was about to cry. "How?" she choked out. "Why?"

"Shifters have a bit more protection from magic than most beings. It's part of what makes us unique among the supernatural races. We can take hits that would destroy most other kinds of folk. The magic sort of rolls off our fur, even when we're not wearing it," Nick explained, finding it hard to find the right words. "It would take a lot for your mom to hurt any of us, even the cubs," he tried to reassure her.

Sal squeezed his hand tight, and a single tear tracked down her soft cheek. He bent to kiss it away, knowing how monumental the past few moments had been for her.

"I'm..." She tried to talk, but it took a couple of tries before her voice would work. "Thank you, Mark. Shelly. I...I don't know what to say." More tears threatened, but they were happy tears. Ecstatic tears.

"I'm glad Mark and my dad could help," Shelly assured Sal. "And I'm certain we're going to be great friends. And probably classmates. I understand we both came to magecraft kind of late in life." Shelly's conspiratorial giggle invited Sal to join in.

"I guess so," Sal agreed, looking at Nick and then turning her gaze to Mark. "That is... If the Alpha agrees to let me stay."

Nick sucked in a breath. Sal had pushed the issue, and he was still somewhat afraid of what Mark would say.

"You're welcome among us, Sal," Mark said formally. "As friend to the Clan. As mate to my best friend, Beta, and protector of the Clan. And as a Clan member in your own right by virtue of that mating."

Nick's breath rushed out in relief. This couldn't have gone better. He wouldn't have to leave his people, and Sal had just gotten a giant-sized welcome from the Alpha. Mark couldn't make it much plainer than that.

Nick held out his hand, drawing Mark in for a back-pounding hug. "Thank you, Mark," he said low, near Mark's ear. "I won't let you down."

Mark stepped back and looked at Nick. "You never have, and you never could. Congratulations on finding your mate."

"Thanks," Nick said, feeling it down to the soles of his feet. He was so grateful to be alive and mated to the most wonderful woman in the world.

Shelly was hugging Sal, and when the two women broke apart, Sal came right back to fit under his outstretched arm. The two couples just stood there for a moment, joy between them.

"I'm going to do the official welcome at dinner," Mark told them. "Try to act surprised."

Sal laughed. "I usually get paid to act," she said, then looked as if she might want to recall those words, but Shelly and Mark laughed with her.

"Speaking of which, you'll be able to keep acting, if that's what you want," Mark told her when the laughter had died down. "I've managed a very public life in the human world, and I think you can, too."

"I hadn't thought about it much, to be honest," Sal admitted. "But, if I still have a career, I might as well take advantage of it while it lasts. As long as I can get a handle on the magic, I might just look into taking on a few roles to build a little nest egg. That is, if Nick doesn't mind."

"Mind?" Nick replied, hugging her to his side. "Why should I mind? As long as you let me run your security, you can go just about anywhere you want, sweetheart."

"Does this mean I'm losing you as my head of security?" Mark asked, but there was a grin on his face.

"You've got enough young jaguars to watch your back when you leave the island," Nick told him. "And I'll go along when I can, but you have to understand, my mate is my first priority now, Mark." Nick looked into Sal's eyes and got lost in the love he saw there.

Mark's words came as if from a distance. "I understand, my friend, and I couldn't be happier for you."

Nick didn't hear if Mark said anything else because he was kissing his mate. As far as he was concerned only the two of them existed on the entire planet.

Shelly and Mark walked away, leaving the two newlyweds to their kisses, but as they tiptoed along the corridor, Shelly put her hand in her mate's. "Do you think we should send someone to get them if they don't surface for a while?"

Mark grinned down at her and shrugged. "If they miss dinner, they can always do a midnight kitchen raid. Nick knows where everything is."

Having done quite a few of those midnight kitchen raids herself over the past few weeks with her new mate, Shelly couldn't help but smile. She hadn't liked Nick when they first met, but she found herself softening toward the man she'd dubbed Atilla the Bodyguard. Sal was a nice woman, and somehow, she softened the hard-assed security chief.

With a shrug, Shelly turned her attention fully to her new husband. "I guess you're right. What do you say we cut this dinner short and raid the kitchen for ice cream around midnight?"

Mark smiled at his adventurous mate. "I'm game if you are."

The official welcome announcement happened the next

day, but nobody really minded. It was clear to everyone in the Clan that the Alpha and Beta couples were lost in love, and the jaguars were incredibly happy. Things were looking up for the Jaguar Clan and the island that they were turning into a true home.

# # #

Thank you for reading **The Jaguar Bodyguard**. If you enjoyed this book, please consider leaving a review.

Howls Romance
Classic romance... with a furry twist!

Did you enjoy this Howls Romance story?
If YES, check out the other books in the Howls Romance line by heading over to our website! HowlsRomance.com.

ABOUT THE AUTHOR

Bianca D'Arc has run a laboratory, climbed the corporate ladder in the shark-infested streets of lower Manhattan, studied and taught martial arts, and earned the right to put a whole bunch of letters after her name, but she's always enjoyed writing more than any of her other pursuits. She grew up and still lives on Long Island, where she keeps busy with an extensive garden, several aquariums full of very demanding fish, and writing her favorite genres of paranormal, fantasy and sci-fi romance.

Bianca loves to hear from readers and can be reached through Twitter (@BiancaDArc), Facebook (BiancaDArcAuthor) or through the various links on her website.

WELCOME TO THE D'ARC SIDE…
WWW.BIANCADARC.COM

OTHER BOOKS BY BIANCA D'ARC

Brotherhood of Blood
One & Only
Rare Vintage
Phantom Desires
Sweeter Than Wine
Forever Valentine
Wolf Hills*
Wolf Quest

Tales of the Were
Lords of the Were
Inferno

Tales of the Were ~
The Others
Rocky
Slade

Tales of the Were ~
String of Fate
Cat's Cradle
King's Throne
Jacob's Ladder
Her Warriors

Tales of the Were ~
Redstone Clan
The Purrfect Stranger
Grif
Red
Magnus
Bobcat
Matt

Tales of the Were ~
Grizzly Cove
All About the Bear
Mating Dance
Night Shift
Alpha Bear
Saving Grace
Bearliest Catch
The Bear's Healing Touch
The Luck of the Shifters
Badass Bear
Loaded for Bear

Tales of the Were ~
Were-Fey Love Story
Lone Wolf
Snow Magic
Midnight Kiss

Tales of the Were ~
Jaguar Island (Howls)
The Jaguar Tycoon
The Jaguar Bodyguard

Gemini Project
Tag Team
Doubling Down

Resonance Mates
Hara's Legacy**
Davin's Quest
Jaci's Experiment
Grady's Awakening

Harry's Sacrifice

Dragon Knights

Daughters of the Dragon
Maiden Flight*
Border Lair
The Ice Dragon**
Prince of Spies***

Dragon Knights ~ Novellas
The Dragon Healer
Master at Arms
Wings of Change

Sons of Draconia
FireDrake
Dragon Storm
Keeper of the Flame
Hidden Dragons

The Sea Captain's Daughter
Book 1: Sea Dragon
Book 2: Dragon Fire
Book 3: Dragon Mates

Guardians of the Dark
Half Past Dead
Once Bitten, Twice Dead
A Darker Shade of Dead
The Beast Within
Dead Alert

StarLords
Hidden Talent
Talent For Trouble
Shy Talent

Jit'Suku Chronicles ~ Arcana
King of Swords
King of Cups
King of Clubs
King of Stars
End of the Line
Diva

Jit'Suku Chronicles ~ Sons of Amber
Angel in the Badlands
Master of Her Heart

StarLords
Hidden Talent
Talent For Trouble
Shy Talent

Gifts of the Ancients
Warrior's Heart

* RT Book Reviews Awards Nominee
** EPPIE Award Winner
*** CAPA Award Winner

The first three Grizzly Cove stories in one place!

Welcome to Grizzly Cove, where bear shifters can be who they are - if the creatures of the deep will just leave them be. Wild magic, unexpected allies, a conflagration of sorcery and shifter magic the likes of which has not been seen in centuries... That's what awaits the peaceful town of Grizzly Cove. That, and love. Lots and lots of love.

This anthology contains:

All About the Bear
Welcome to Grizzly Cove, where the sheriff has more than the peace to protect. The proprietor of the new bakery in town is clueless about the dual nature of her nearest neighbors, but not for long. It'll be up to Sheriff Brody to clue her in and convince her to stay calm—and in his bed—for the next fifty years or so.

Mating Dance
Tom, Grizzly Cove's only lawyer, is also a badass grizzly bear, but he's met his match in Ashley, the woman he just can't get out of his mind. She's got a dark secret, that only he knows. When ugliness from her past tracks her to her new home, can Tom protect the woman he is fast coming to believe is his mate?

Night Shift
Sheriff's Deputy Zak is one of the few black bear shifters in a colony of grizzlies. When his job takes him into closer proximity to the lovely Tina, though, he finds he can't resist her. Could it be he's finally found his mate? And when adversity strikes, will she turn to him, or run into the night? Zak will do all he can to make sure she chooses him.

Made in the USA
San Bernardino, CA
20 January 2018